Barry Yourgrau

Another A NASTY book

The Curse of
the Tweeties

(An Entire Novel)

Art by Robert DeJesus

JOANNA COTLER BOOKS
An Imprint of HarperCollins Publishers

Library of Congress Cataloging-in-Publication Data
Yourgrau, Barry.
    Another nastybook : the curse of the Tweeties / Barry Yourgrau.— 1st ed.
        p.   cm.
    Summary: When his mother is kidnapped by goblins, Rollo, inspired by his favorite
comic book character, Su-ichi Samurai Swordboy, embarks on a rescue mission to
Fairyland, aided by imaginary friends, including a set of talking false teeth.
    ISBN-10: 0-06-057981-1 (trade bdg.) — ISBN-13: 978-0-06-057981-4 (trade bdg.)
    ISBN-10: 0-06-057982-X (lib. bdg.) — ISBN-13: 978-0-06-057982-1 (lib. bdg.)
    [1. Adventure and adventurers—Fiction. 2. Heroes—Fiction. 3. Humorous stories.]
I. Title.
PZ7.Y8959Ano 2006   2005017921
[Fic]—dc22   CIP
                                                                            AC

Typography by Neil Swaab
1 2 3 4 5 6 7 8 9 10
❖
First Edition

To Anya, who's still trying to stop me

One

The sun is going down.

It's the lovely end of a long summer's afternoon out at Pleasant Lake.

Just the perfect setting for an early-supper family picnic, and then for sitting around, smiling sappily, as the fireflies come out twinkling in the gathering darkness.

Of course it's also the perfect setting for terror, horror, and bloodcurdling tragedy to strike.

But we get ahead of ourselves.

The kid of this picnicking family, named Rollo, hunches out of sight behind a tree, sneaking bites of a pre-supper NuttiNutz Bar ("The

Treat That's Shockingly Sweet") and rereading his favorite Japanese *manga* action comic book.

Then his mother's voice finds him.

"Rollo!" nags the voice. "Are you hiding over there, with some candy? You'll ruin your appetite—and candy's just not good for you! And d'you think the table's going to set itself, Rollo?"

So Rollo has to hurriedly wipe his mouth, and conceal his NuttiNutz Bar. And reluctantly and carefully close his comic book. And then trudge over to the picnic table with its piles of plates, forks and knives, napkins, etc., all waiting to be unpiled and set out in proper order.

But no, this deprivation and drudgery is not the terror, horror, and tragedy we meant.

"Ooh," sneers Rollo's older sister, whose name is Noreen. "Sneaking a gorge fest before supper? With your piggy nose stuck in that stupid comic, *Suzie Samurai* or whatever?"

"It's *Su-ichi*," snarls Rollo at his sister's deliberate and provocative mangling of facts. "And *he's* not a *regular* samurai, *he's*—"

"Okay, knock it off," growls their dad from the barbecue grill. "You're giving me a headache!"

He coughs, waving at the fatty clouds of burger smoke.

"It's *Su-ichi Samurai Swordboy*!" hisses Rollo, for his obnoxious sister's information. Not that she comprehends in the slightest.

And then all three of them whip their heads around, at Mom's scream from the family van. They see her kicking at something behind the open back door in the dimness.

"What is it?" cries Dad.

Mom comes marching back over toward the picnic table, carrying her "family favorite" banana crème pie. "Some disgusting little creature, with a face like an ugly old man, tried to snatch a bite of my pie!" she exclaims. She chuckles snidely. "But I gave it a kick it'll remember for a long time! It smelled, too, like a skunk."

"A *skunk*?" says Rollo, peering with a mix of fascination and disgust.

"Probably not a skunk, more likely a *possum* with that kind of face," announces Noreen. "Yuck, they carry *rabies*."

"Rabies, you're always whining about *rabies*!" sneers Rollo.

"Will you two *stop* bickering!" declares Mom.

"My headache," coughs Dad.

"We're ready to eat," says Mom. "Why's the lantern not lit? Rollo?"

And on this typical note of parents nagging and siblings squabbling, the family picnic supper begins by charming Pleasant Lake at sunset.

And perhaps the terror, horror, and tragedy occurs now—in the form of Dad's black-charred burgers and turkey franks, and Mom's weird potato salad containing gummy carrot scrapings and squishy, revolting, bug-sized raisins, which Rollo and Noreen furtively scrape out and quarantine in disgust at the sides of their plates.

But no, this isn't what we meant, not even when eagle-eyed Mom says, "Hey, you two, I see what you're up to with your raisins!" Nor when she starts slicing her "family favorite" banana crème pie, whose unique lumpiness the family is subjected to several times a year, on happy family occasions like this. "Boy, did I ever give that ugly creature a kick," Mom chuckles again, with a shake of her head.

"You know, rabies can be transmitted—"

"Noreen, we're *eating*!" protests grossed-out Rollo.

"Stop already!" grumbles Dad, his mouth full.

"Boy, just look at 'em!" sighs Mom; and she smiles, gazing out at the myriad of fireflies twinkling wondrously in the gathering darkness beyond the lantern light of the picnic table. The whole family gazes together. . . .

And a long twinkling hush falls, there by Pleasant Lake. . . .

Too bad it doesn't last.

Mom sniffs.

"Hey . . ." she says slowly.

The whole family twist their heads about. "What a smell—" blurts Noreen.

Out of nowhere a violent gust of wind buffets the picnic table. Then another, sending the dessert paper plates flying, and knocking over the lantern. The family shouts. All the fireflies seem to disappear at once; thunder rumbles. The wind lashes the family picnic table in fury.

Mom and Noreen shriek as a horde of

midget two-legged creatures comes boiling and grappling out of the sudden darkness. They have the faces of weird little old men, with long wrinkly ears and far-apart eyes, with wide wrinkly cheeks and sharp noses. They wear bushy jackets made of leaves and flowers!

"How dare you abuse one of our goblin kind?" they squawk, high-pitched and oddly old-fashioned sounding. Many little hands seize hold of flailing Mom, and start dragging her away off her picnic bench.

"Help, help!" bleats Mom.

"Hey, stop!" shouts Dad, floundering on the ground behind his bench, where he's keeled over.

"Mom!" wails Noreen. "Oh, Mom!"

"See how she likes a nice little stay in Fairyland!" cackles a tiny vicious voice out of the throng, as the kidnappers disappear into the inky, stormy evening.

And *this* is our terror, horror, and bloodcurdling tragedy, yes indeed. Understand now?

Rollo stares blinking into the buffeting wind. His face breaks into an amazed grin.

"Wow . . ." he blurts. *"Cool!"*

Rollo, you see, represents the viewpoint of your action-adventure comic book fan.

His dad swarms to his feet at last, and gapes into the wind himself. But not grinning. "Hurry!" he gasps. He turns and rushes over to the barbecue grill, which is lying on its side. He starts hauling it toward the van. "Let's get out of here before they kidnap us!" he shouts.

Rollo stares as his sister goes scrounging for the plates and silverware, which have spilled into the grass.

"Don't forget the lantern!" his dad calls back.

"But—what about Mom?" Rollo protests, in confusion. He twists about toward where he last saw her. "Aren't we gonna *rescue* her?"

Two

It's two hours later.

"But aren't we gonna *rescue* Mom?"

Rollo repeats his question for the fourth time, as he plods around to the rear of the van to help his dad unload the grill. They're back in their driveway at home. "How can we just desert her?"

"Rollo, that's the fourth time you've asked both questions!" grunts his dad. "Don't you listen? Your mother will be fine, just fine, you know how she is. Chasing after her will only screw things up worse!"

"Like *you* always do," sneers Noreen, going

up the back steps to the kitchen door with the picnic basket and what's left of the dishes and such.

"But shouldn't we at least call the police?" asks Rollo, a little weakly because it's the third time he's asked.

"For the fourth time, *no*!" snaps his dad, miscounting unfairly.

"What would police know about *Fairyland*?" snorts Noreen.

"How long d'you think I'd stay in the real estate business, if my customers found out my wife'd been kidnapped by fairies?"

"Goblins," mutters Rollo. "But—"

"Dad?" says Noreen. "Till Mom gets back, can I wear that new orange blouse she just got?"

"Sure, sure," shrugs Dad. "Whatever."

Rollo stares at them. They turn away, oblivious.

"But that's *Mom's hat*," Rollo exclaims to his sister, staring again, an hour later.

It's just before bedtime and he's standing at the doorway of Noreen's room, under the GIRLS

RULE! sign. Noreen has on their mom's prize souvenir pink baseball cap, from the family outing last year to Roaring Rainbows theme park.

"It happens to look much better on me," sniffs Noreen. "And what's it to you, anyway, Dad doesn't mind!"

"But it's not right," scowls Rollo. Their own mother's been carried off, and no one lifts a finger? "What if the goblins, you know, torture her or something?"

"Oh, *please.* They'll probably just ransom her for a lot of money. And then we'll have to sell the house, and live in poverty, and walk everywhere. But knowing Mom, they'll probably pay us to take her back in a day or two!"

"Hey, quiet out there!" calls their father's sleepy voice from down the hall in the master bedroom.

"*Anyway,*" whispers Noreen, violently, "since when are you so big on Mom? Last week you said she should go back to Mars when she made you clean your room. So now you've got nothing to worry about," she snorts. "So why don't you just creep back to your pigsty and stuff your fat face with one of your candy bars!"

Which is very unkind, of course, because Rollo isn't fat, he just prefers candy bars to all other forms of foodstuffs.

Then she slams the door.

"Hey, *quiet*."

Rollo lies awake in the dark, permanent shambles that are his room, and chomps on a NuttiNutz Bar, and broods. He sees again the gross little wrinkly faces and grabbing hands of the smelly goblins, and he imagines his mom undergoing some of the terrifying ill treatments on display in the pages of *Su-ichi Samurai Swordboy*! "Cowards," he whispers, about his father and sister. *"Most cravenly cowards,"* he adds, this being the sort of terminology he's picked up from his *manga* comics.

Maybe they'll find their courage tomorrow, he hopes.

But at breakfast his dad just grunts over the newspaper, as usual. Then he mumbles, "Okay, be good." Then he leaves for work.

That's it.

Noreen spends the rest of the morning rummaging in their mom's closet, as if at a bargain sale at the mall. Rollo stares at her through the window from the backyard. He stares during breaks while practicing samurai stick fighting, which consists of hacking and whacking at a dying pine tree with his plastic street-hockey stick. By way of a samurai kimono he wears an oversized professional ice-hockey uniform shirt: the Jellyfish, specifically. Rollo plays street hockey sometimes with his buddies, who mock him for his shirt, because the Jellyfish were such a dopey team before going out of business. But his buddies are all gone now for the summer.

No ransom note shows up in the afternoon. No ransom phone call from a weird little old-fashioned voice. No Mom.

And an idea begins to form in Rollo's mind, perhaps as the result of so much sugar in his diet and his fantastical reading habits. A crazy idea, growing as Rollo hacks away at his pine tree. Crazy, yes. But undeniably exciting . . .

At dinner (rewarmed take-out chicken) Rollo's dad takes a big swig of his beer and clears his throat, and says, "So I was thinking, that if your mom isn't back in a day or two, maybe I might invite Mrs. Schnockler from across the street to join us for supper. Just for company."

"Didn't she just get divorced?" says Noreen.

"Oh, did she? I don't keep up with those things," says Dad, in the phoniest way imaginable. Then he turns red and takes a giant swig of beer.

"Dad, I'm wearing these earrings of Mom's now? But can I also borrow these?"

Rollo, mouth full of drumstick, looks at his greedy sister holding up a pile of jewelry. And right then inspiration hits full force. He is no hero—he swallows—*but a heroic call has come to him.*

"Just like Su-ichi Samurai Swordboy!" he announces to Noreen in a magnificent whisper, at her door at bedtime. "When the Jade Monkey Princess was carried off by the Robot Reptiles."

"Huh?" says Noreen. Her diamond-crusted ears sagging.

"Don't you understand?" demands Rollo,

exasperated. "I'm going on a heroic quest—to rescue Mom from Fairyland! Since you and Dad are cravenly cowards."

Noreen sneers, stung. "Ooh, aren't we courageous and noble and high-minded all of a sudden," she snorts. "How're you gonna even find Fairyland? You have a terrible sense of direction."

"It's probably right there by Pleasant Lake somewhere."

"It won't be by Pleasant Lake, we'd have heard about it before!"

"Well, I'll find it," Rollo promises. "Maybe a guide will help me—like the old blind Dragon Scout who helped Su-ichi Samurai Swordboy!"

"You're pathetic," Noreen informs him. "I'm telling Dad."

"*Why?* You want that awful Mrs. Schnockler hanging around?"

"Quiet . . ." grumbles their father's drowsy voice down the hall.

"Why not? I can get tips on how to flirt from her."

"You tell Dad," hisses Rollo, "and I'll tell

him about the liquor cabinet in April, and that half a cigarette behind the pine tree!"

"You're *pathetic*!" hisses Noreen.

"Hey, *quiet . . .*" calls the sleepy voice.

"And you'll just screw everything up, *like you always do*! I hope the goblins tear you to little pieces!"

Then she slams her door.

"Quiet!"

Wouldn't it be great to have an older sister who was supportive, and gave you a nice encouraging send-off when you were about to undertake a perilous quest to rescue your beloved parent (okay, more or less beloved) and restore your family to the wholesome, loving bunch they are at heart?

This is what Rollo thinks, too, as he tosses about on his pillow, waiting for dawn. But never mind! He can't fall asleep, mainly because he ate two whole NuttiNutz Bars in excitement before turning off the light. His mind is aflame with images of upcoming heroics, of his valiant deeds. Where will Fairyland prove to be? High among the clouds, like the Ghost Demon

Assassins' hidden fortress? Down in a dreary bottomless cave abyss, "where the Robot Reptiles lurk," as in the Jade Monkey Princess saga?

Maybe there'll be a comic book based on his exploits? he wonders. He gulps, tingling. Or even a movie, maybe? Not that he's conceited, of course.

But where exactly *is* Fairyland? *Where . . . ?*

He wakes up suddenly. Gray light seeps through the blinds. Dawn already?

He struggles up, yawning. He creeps groggily downstairs through the sleeping house. He carries his backpack, containing a supply of candy bars, his *Su-ichi Samurai Swordboy* comic book, and his Jellyfish pro-hockey uniform shirt, to be donned for actual combat with the enemy. In his hand he bears his street-hockey samurai stick.

And you might wonder, what chance does a semidelusional suburban kid stoked on candy bars and armed only with a piece of plastic sports equipment have of rescuing anyone kidnapped anywhere in the world, let alone Fairyland?

Well, you'd be right to wonder! But you know comic book fans—they get the absurdest

notions in their heads. *They just do not appreciate reality.*

So out he sneaks into the snoozing streets,
on his high-minded quest to rescue his mom
who's been carried off by goblins enraged by her
actions when one of them tried to sneak a taste
of banana crème pie. . . .

Our hero, Rollo Samurai Stickboy!

Three

So where *is* Fairyland?

Brave young Rollo has a plan to find out. Delusional and reckless he may be. But he's not a fool altogether. Not at all.

Instead of heading to the bus station and trying to figure out the schedules and connections up to Pleasant Lake and then just blundering around up there, Rollo is going to seek the guidance of someone who might know.

Last night he remembered about the very strange magic store he saw, the time his dad took him along on a real-estate appointment. His dad wouldn't stop because they were "on business and couldn't fool around." But Rollo had always wanted to go back.

It was way downtown . . . somewhere. . . .

For a couple of hours, Rollo sleepily tramps the grimy downtown sidewalks. At last, along a dreary crooked side street, almost hidden away, he spots what must be the store. At least he thinks it is. Though it looks very different now from what he remembered. He stands opposite, staring, the last chomp of a breakfast NuttiNutz in his mouth.

OTHER REALMS . . . AND BEYOND

reads the sign in the window, almost obscured behind a line of dangling little colorful banners with Japanese letters. Everything's in shadow under the long jutting eaves of the peculiar curved wooden roof.

Just like the Ghost Demon Assassins' fake-temple hideout in *Su-ichi Samurai Swordboy*!

"Jeepers," whispers Rollo, astonished and thrilled. He gulps, and with his heart pounding he grips his hockey stick hard, and ducks under the banners to the store's front door. He turns the intricately carved handle, and with a swallow, he steps inside.

"Jeepers!" he exclaims again (what can you do, that's how he talks). *"Coolness!"* He stares at a huge room full of shadows and shafts of dusty sunlight slanting from high windows. Deep, cobwebbed shelves extend far into the dimness left and right, and all about are crude wooden tables and benches.

Why, the inside is an exact replica of the Ghost Demon Assassins' tavern headquarters!

"Yes-s-s?" demands a voice, in a slow, booming whisper.

Rollo peers and sees a man seated behind a high counter at the back. The man is plump, with long flowing white hair and a long flowing forked beard. The black silk of his kimono gleams.

"What is it you want?" he booms, and his eyes glitter under his tangled snowy eyebrows.

Rollo regrips his hockey stick with both hands. He realizes, strangely but marvelously, that he is now wearing his Jellyfish uniform shirt, even though he can't remember putting it on.

"I'm R-Rollo," he begins; and then his

wavering young voice grows firm and bold, and he takes a step forward, hockey stick proudly clutched. "Rollo Samurai Stickboy!" he cries. "Perhaps you've heard of me! I'm on a glorious quest to rescue my beloved mom from Fairyland, where the goblins took her. Cravenly cowardly are my sister and father," he cries, very heroically. "So how do I find it, please? Fairyland, I mean."

The plump man blinks his jade-green eyes under their wild brows. Slowly he tips back his fat pale head, and he laughs, so the prongs of his beard dance like snakes. Then he leans forward, grinning with blackened, pointy teeth, and he says:

"Stupid brave Rollo Samurai Stickboy! Fairyland you'll never get to! 'Cause we'll cut you up into a thousand pieces first!"

Again he laughs, and claps his fat pale hands.

A horde of Assassins spring up from behind the tables where they've been hiding! Rollo gasps. They're all very small and wrinkly and look just like the goblins at Pleasant Lake, except they have long snowy forked beards and wear little black kimonos. Their samurai swords flash.

Heart thumping under his Jellyfish shirt, out-numbered Rollo sets himself to face his attackers. Suddenly the nearest Assassin shrieks hysterically, and charges, sword raised high. Rollo squawks, but coolly, and swings his samurai stick with all his might—there's a hollow wooden clunk, like the sound of the pine tree when he whacks it. The attacker's little head goes flying off and rolls away against the foot of a bench. Rollo gapes. Everyone gapes. An awful smell rises.

"Yuck," snorts Rollo.

Then everyone screams insanely, and charges.

Frantically Rollo thrusts his hockey stick forward and spears an Assassin in the chest. He lifts the wriggling kimonoed figure up high in the air, and starts twirling him around and around like the head of a whirling hammer, knocking Assassins flying in all directions.

"This's the *double coolest!*" whoops Rollo—and then he whips his hockey stick like a cata-pult, sending the speared Assassin flying through the air like a living bowling ball that crashes into what's left of the attacking horde, ricocheting off one then another then another, knocking mini-Assassins senseless back into the splintering tables, down into the upturned benches, up into the collapsing shelves.

Rollo stands gaping at the wreckage, chest heaving. A big disbelieving grin spreads across his face. "Whew," he grimaces, "what a smell!"

"Well, well, *well*," declares the man behind the counter. "Look at *you*. But you'll still never get to Fairyland—'cause you still have to tangle with *me*!"

And with shocking agility he leaps up onto the counter, and assumes a froglike fighting stance, and raises the great glittering blade of his samurai doomsword. He laughs, black teethed. Then he reaches up over across the top of his head and seizes one of his ears, and slowly— unbelievably—he pulls off his head! A second head is revealed, exactly the same, only smaller.

"Spooky, huh?" he cackles.

And then he flings the old crumply head at Rollo and leaps off the counter to attack.

The flapping, bearded head comes bouncing toward Rollo; just as it reaches him, he swings his hockey stick, street-hockey style, and blasts a mighty slap shot that would be the envy of his hockey tormenter, Alvin Olson, sending the head rocketing back. The whirling head slams right into the onrushing attacker's kimonoed chest. In great surprise his current face stares down at his former face, as he's sent hurtling backward, zooming all the way to the counter, where he crashes and explodes in a fat shower of a million kimonoed fragments!

"*Wow* . . ." gasps Rollo.

What a sensational time he's having at this samurai stuff. What a tremendous natural talent he seems to have for being on a quest! Really, he's just as good as Su-ichi Samurai Swordboy. (Maybe even a little better?)

"Rollo? Oh, Rollo, is that you?"

A familiar voice is calling. "Oh, brave Rollo, I was so wrong about you!"

"Mom?" cries Rollo, peering around. "Mom, is that you?" And he spots her, way at the back with a broom, starting to clean up the big reeking mess.

"Of course it's me," cries his mom. "Oof, this smell!"

"But weren't you carried off to Fairyland?" exclaims Rollo, confused.

"Oh, don't always be asking questions, Rollo," snaps his mother. "But I'm so *proud* of you, Samurai Stickboy, that I'm going to allow you not to clean your room for two whole months. What do you say to that? And you can have all the NuttiNutz Bars you want, within reason."

"Thanks, Mom!" cries Rollo, beaming but modest. Effortlessly he bounds toward her, over the wrecked furniture and the vanquished stinking foe, with each joyful step applause rises all around him, swelling louder and louder, until it turns into something more like *knocking*, like someone slowly *knocking* on a huge door, really intrusive and annoying and *earsplitting*.

"Hey!" protests Rollo furiously—

and his eyes blink open.

Noreen stands sneering down at him in his bedroom doorway. In broad daylight.

"It's almost eleven o'clock," she announces. "Weren't you going to rescue Mom? You're so full of hot air, as always!"

four

Yes, all of Rollo's heroics were just a dream. Afraid so. Not to be critical, but what do you expect after consuming a couple of candy bars at bedtime? Seriously, do you think any disciplined samurai or samurai swordboy would gobble down NuttiNutz at that hour? A diet like that? Doubtful. Seriously doubtful!

Anyway.

"Uh . . ." blinks stunned Rollo, there in his bed.

"So I'm going to the mall now with Renee, to practice flirting," Noreen informs him. "Then we're coming back here to gossip. So don't leave all your putrid mess all over the kitchen, *okay*? And *don't* blather to Renee about Mom being kidnapped by goblins, it's so . . . *Rollo*."

And she slams the door.

Cursing, Rollo struggles up. He scrambles into his clothes and clatters downstairs through the empty house (his dad's long off at work) with his backpack and hockey stick. At the front door, he stops. Defiantly, he puts on his Jellyfish uniform shirt. Then he heads out down the front steps, yawning, to commence his brave quest, for real.

He yawns so prodigiously he almost runs headfirst into Mrs. Schnockler, who's out walking her little white toy poodle, Snowflake.

"Oh, hello, Raleigh," she smiles, swaying on high heels in a cloud of perfume. "Off to a hockey game?"

"It's—*Rollo*," sputters Rollo, who hates his name said wrongly. And he's thrown into confusion, because Mrs. Schnockler changes her hair color so often, it's bizarre. "And actually— actually—"

But his pronouncement is drowned by Snowflake's inane frantic barking. "Well, byedy bye, say hi to your dad! Oh, and your mom too, of course," cries Mrs. Schnockler. And she sways off at the end of Snowflake's straining leash.

In a huff, Rollo turns and stamps away. The thought of Mrs. Schnockler at the family dinner table refires his valorous resolve. Of course many people might side with his father about Mrs. Schnockler, but that's another matter.

Downtown, after much tramping, Rollo manages to find the magic shop. At least he's fairly sure it's the one. It doesn't resemble his dream at all, though the side street *is* dreary. Creepy even . . . creepier than how he thought he remembered it.

Magyck & Fantasye Noveltyes Worlde

reads the faded lettering in the grimy, vaguely familiar front window. Rollo stands studying it, gnawing on a breakfast NuttiNutz Bar. (We're not saying anything.) He grips his hockey stick. Taking a deep breath, he strides up to the front door, and turns the handle.

A little bell tinkles above his head as he peers inside. It really is a shop this time, not the Ghost Demon Assassins' tavern headquarters, certainly to look at: rows of dusty shelves and a lot of dingy, cutesy knickknacks.

"Yeah?" says a sour, high-pitched voice.

A scrawny old man at a desk off to one side glares around at Rollo. He wears old-style wire-rimmed spectacles, through which his scowl of annoyance seems permanent. "What d'you want, kid?" he pipes.

Stepping in, Rollo takes a deep bold breath to reply—and then he starts sneezing and coughing because of his dust allergy. "I'm Rollo—Sam—Stickboy!" he gasps. "Can you please—tell me—where's Fairy—my mom's—" cough cough cough!

"Can I *what*?" says the old man.

"My mom—" coughs Rollo. "The goblins stole her!" He swallows laboriously. "And they took her to Fairyland. And I'm on a bold quest to rescue her. Can you please tell me where it is? Fairyland, I mean?"

A look of pain spreads across the old man's

face. The bell tinkles for another customer, who enters and after pausing, wanders among the shelves. "Kid, you been reading too many weird books," says the owner scornfully. "There is no Fairyland, sonny, didn't anyone tell you? It's all make-believe. It's play play!"

Which is not a very supportive thing to say to someone on his first valiant quest. Certainly not in the tone of voice you'd use on a kindergartner.

"That's not true," Rollo cries. "Out at Pleasant Lake, the goblins—"

"Hey! This is a novelty shop, see? So whyn't you *buy* yourself a fun set of fake false teeth? They chatter all by themselves, like they're cold. Or a nice Celtic scented candle, for when your mom gets back. Or even a book—there must be some old fairy tales somewheres here."

"Where?" says Rollo, and he turns about to look.

"Watch the hockey stick!" cries the owner. "You break anything, you pay for—" On cue, something crashes to the floor right by Rollo. The scrawny old man leaps to his feet. Rollo swings around to see what broke and there's another crash. "My God, those are ceramic scented candleholders!" squawks the owner. "Do you know how much they cost?"

Rollo learns the answer to this when he's forced to fork over an outrageous amount from the money he brought along from his savings, which was hidden at the bottom of his laundry-infested closet. And then he's shooed outside, and the front door bangs shut after him.

And there our would-be hero stands on the street, blinking in his Jellyfish hockey shirt, a dim look on his red face. He can't believe it. His courageous mission has been shockingly disre-spected! Su-ichi Samurai Swordboy was never treated like this, never! Of course Su-ichi Samurai Swordboy never went into a shop with a lot of breakable items.

But what's he supposed to do now, how's he going to find out where Fairyland is? Just blun-der around by Pleasant Lake, hoping maybe to bump into some goblins? What happened to his wonderful dream?

Whining, this is called.

"Hey, kid," a whispered voice hisses.

Rollo turns, and peers: a man dressed in a dark, shabby coat creeps from the shadows of a doorway down the sidewalk. "I heard you speak of goblins in there," he says, talking low. "Want to get to Fairyland, do you? Maybe I can help you."

"You *can*?" says Rollo. A thrill goes through him. Because this stranger is wearing an actual eye patch, too; and a long moustache droops past his narrow bony chin.

"But first, the vital question," whispers the stranger. *"Got any more money?"*

"M-maybe . . ." says Rollo, who knows enough to be suspicious of such questions.

"I'll take that as a yes," grins the stranger. "Well, then, let's go eat! Well, come on, come on, let's not loiter!" he says. And with an anxious glance over his shoulder back toward the magic shop, he steers Rollo around the corner.

Five

"A *quest*, eh?" says the eye-patched stranger, his mouth full, examining Rollo up and down with his good eye. "Well, you're a foolhardy kid, Raleigh, but a mighty brave one, I'll hand ya that." He swallows noisily and crams another enormous load of syrup-saturated waffles into his mouth.

"It's Rollo." But Rollo's cheeks glow from the praise. How great to get support for his quest instead of sneers!

The two of them sit in a booth far in the shadowy rear of a dim, cobwebbed diner. The stranger, whose name doesn't really suit his appearance ("Marvin Tweetie; but you can call me Marv"), has already gone through several plates of waffles. He has two more in front of him now. Rollo has never seen someone eat so voraciously, especially someone so skinny. Rollo is extremely impressed with Marv Tweetie, despite his name and his limited samurai knowledge. Because he seems to know a lot about candy bars. The topic came up when they sat down.

"Three NuttiNutz Bars at one time, you say?" Marv Tweetie had scoffed. "I once ate seven ChooeyGooeys in row, kid. *Seven. Plus* a couple of NuttiNutz."

Not that candy is all they've talked about, to be fair to their sense of priorities. Rollo has explained all about the kidnapping at Pleasant Lake. And the craven cowardliness of his dad and Noreen, especially how vile and personally insulting Noreen has been.

"She said going after Mom I'd screw things up, 'like I always do'!" he protests. "Can you believe that? Know what she and her friend Renee Duffman once did to me? They stole—"

"Yeah, *older sisters*," Marv Tweetie interrupts, muttering. He rubs at his syrupy moustache and chin with a saturated napkin. "I know all about *older sisters*." He reaches for the little pitcher of syrup. It's empty. "Hey, waiter, more syrup!"

Then he glances back nervously out the window, as he's been doing all along.

"That's five syrups you gone through!" grumbles the waiter, coming over.

"So what, the kid'll pay, the kid'll pay," retorts Marv Tweetie, giving a toss of his shabby black coat. He pours most of the new pitcher over the big mess on his plates and resumes greedily.

The mention of "pay" prompts Rollo to get back to business. "So how," he whispers intently, "how can I get to Fairyland?"

"We'll get to that, we'll get to that," mumbles Marv Tweetie, syrup-glazed cheeks restuffed. "First the meal, then the deal, eh?"

"But how *do* you know about goblins and things?" persists Rollo, purposeful and also now a little bewildered at the amount Marv Tweetie is consuming.

"Well, Raleigh," he replies, and he lowers his

voice, which makes his words even harder to understand as his long moustache tips flip about with his labors, "I'm what . . . they call . . . an *adventurer*." He strains mightily, and swallows. "At great personal risk," he pants, "I acquire objects of immeasurable value to others, in the pursuit of their mighty ends and purposes!"

Which is exactly the sort of mumbo jumbo someone on a quest, like Rollo, wants to hear.

"*Co-o-ol.*"

"But it'll cost ya, it'll cost ya," warns Marv Tweetie, gloating happily. He shovels up more waffle mess and then glances again nervously out the window. When he turns back, a thought seems to cross his mind, as he works the new load in his jaws. He nods at Rollo's hockey stick. "Your samurai whatchamacallit there. Pretty good with it, are you?"

What a question! Rollo proudly informs him all about his swordboy-style backyard practice sessions. "And I just had the *wildest* dream about it," he announces. Because who doesn't like boring people with their dreams at the slightest opportunity?

Marv Tweetie listens, munching and burping along softly. He doesn't seem entirely bored. "Quite a dream," he murmurs, when Rollo's done. And then slowly he cocks his head, and stares one-eyed at Rollo . . . very strangely.

"W-what?" says Rollo.

Marv Tweetie just smiles, beckoning him to lean close. Uncertainly Rollo does, staring back at the single glaring eye, at the eye patch, which shows little splatters of syrup.

"Who says," whispers Marv Tweetie, smiling evilly, darkly, bizarrely, "*who says you're not . . . STILL DREAMING?*

"WHO SAYS?" he roars, his stuffed mouth wailing, his arms bursting up and flapping like a buzzard from hell in his black shabby coat.

Rollo screams, heaving back in his seat. Spastically he clutches for his samurai hockey stick.

"Hey, you creep, why're you scaring the kid!" demands the waiter, appearing suddenly. He leans in and seizes Marv Tweetie by the scruff of his collar.

"It's a joke, it's a joke!" squawks Marv

Tweetie. "I was just testing him—"

"Yeah? I'll test you," snarls the waiter, twisting him a foot off his seat.

"Explain, Raleigh—explain—" bleats the joker.

"It was a joke?" pants Rollo. Shakily, he grins.

"Yeah?" says the waiter. He releases Marv Tweetie, who thuds back down. "Okay, you two, so just pay up and get going, you and your sick jokes been here long enough. And move your hockey stick, kid, someone's gonna trip over it!"

"Yes, better go pay," gasps Marv Tweetie. He doesn't look well at all.

Rollo goes off to the cash register. It costs an awful lot! Plus he winds up paying for several earlier bills of Marv Tweetie's. Then he has to visit the restroom, to wipe off the stains on his Jellyfish shirt from syrupy spraying and roaring.

He goes back to the table angrily. But Marv Tweetie looks just dreadful. He's slumped in his seat, his skin a ghastly green, huge drops of perspiration beaded on his face.

"I ate too much . . ." he puffs.

"I'll say, you had five whole plates of waf-fles!" scowls Rollo. "Plus I had to pay—"

"Kid, I'm a goner," gasps Marv Tweetie. "I'm not gonna make it."

"What d'you mean?" says Rollo, eyes widening.

"But I'll give you . . . what you need . . . to find Fairyland. Gonna cost . . . $50,000. No? Okay . . . $12.78?"

"Okay," gulps Rollo, mentally calculating expenses. "What is it? I'll—I'll go get change."

"Ah, never mind," gasps Marv Tweetie fee-bly, good eye fallen shut. He instructs Rollo to reach in under his coat. Rollo finds a small card-board box. It's light.

"Want me to call a doctor?" he asks, staring, when he's put the box away in his backpack as instructed.

Marv Tweetie laughs softly, in agony. "Too late for that. I think my stomach's exploded."

"Wow, *gross*," whispers Rollo. "But *cool*, too—but *gross*!" he blurts, as a dribble of lethal sludge oozes out at the corner of Marv Tweetie's lips.

"Better get going, Raleigh, before it's too . . .

look out the window, kid, tell me if anyone's . . .
coming."

Rollo gulps, and peers out—straight into the
back of head of the owner of the magic shop,
who's peering about this way and that on the
sidewalk. Who suddenly wheels around and
gapes right at Rollo.

"You!" he squawks, pointing a bony, wrath-
ful finger. *"Thieves!"* He rushes off down toward
the diner entrance.

"It's the guy from the shop!" cries Rollo.

"Run for it, kid, run for it," mumbles expir-
ing Marv Tweetie.

But Rollo's hockey stick is jammed under his
seat. By the time he wrenches it free, the owner
has come charging up through the booths. "Pair
of shoplifters! Where's my merchandise?"

An awkwardly vicious, syrup-sticky struggle
explodes. Rollo tries to whack with his stick,
samurai-style, but the scrawny oldster is much
fiercer than you'd expect. He seizes control of
Rollo's samurai stick from him, and bangs Rollo
on the head with the blade.

"Ow! Ow!" yelps Rollo.

"Get him, Raleigh!" whispers Marv Tweetie, faintly.

"You creep, quit abusing that kid!" roars the waiter, rushing up. He seizes the old man in a crunching headlock.

"Run, Raleigh, run—" blurts Marv Tweetie, and then he gurgles, horrifically.

Rollo wriggles around the heaving strugglers, making sure to stamp on the old man's spectacles, which have fallen off. This is a pretty cowardly act of payback, but who cares? He scrambles away for the diner exit. Down into the street, off around the corner he races, with his hockey stick and his backpack with its precious contents.

On and on Rollo gallops, block after block, checking back to see if he's being chased. Heads turn to watch him chug by. Several people yell mocking remarks about the Jellyfish, but Rollo's heard most of them before.

At last he sees a little neighborhood park, and he lumbers into it, scattering pigeons a fat old lady is feeding. He scrambles into the cover of a clump of bushes. There, panting and gasping, he flings himself onto his knees. The old pigeon lady stands scowling over in his general direction. Rollo looks left and right; then he brings the precious cardboard box out of his backpack. He rubs his sore head where his own hockey samurai stick clanked him. Then with trembling hands, he very carefully opens the box lid.

Very carefully, he peers in.

Inside the box is a set of false teeth. Fake, plastic ones.

"Hi, guess you're Raleigh?" they declare. "Something about a quest?"

xiꝛ

Now, how would *you* react to being addressed by a bunch of disembodied big white joke choppers, grinning in bright pink gums—and that's all?

"*Co-o-ol.* I guess. . . ." is how Rollo reacts, with a gulp.

A grin of his own wobbles across his face; a very bewildered, uncertain sort of grin. While his mouth hangs open.

"How about a little air?" say the false teeth. "Gimme a hand out, will ya, Raleigh?"

"It's Rollo," murmurs Rollo, as hesitantly he reaches into the box to oblige.

"Ooh, that tickles!" yelp the teeth.

Rollo wiggles them out, and sets them on top of a tree stump. Then he snatches his hands back out of biting range, instinctively.

"Ah, much better! Stuffy in there. And that store shelf, whew, *dusty*."

Rollo stares. The teeth must be an oracle, which is incredibly exciting. But they're very different from the Whispering Rock oracle behind the waterfall, for instance, which was a great source of info about Robot Reptiles for you-know-who Swordboy. This oracle seems awfully . . . *unconventional*.

"So how come you can speak?" asks Rollo, not being all that diplomatic.

"Oh, I dunno," reply the joke dentures airily, with a little laugh that reeks of false modesty. "Guess I always had a talent!"

"So can other ones from the store speak too?"

"Excuse me? Of course *not*!" clack the false teeth. They're highly offended, there on their stump. "So anyway, what's on your mind, Raleigh?"

"It's Rollo." Surely an oracle should get your name right!

"Rolleigh."

"Rollo."

"Rahlo!"

"Rollo!!"

"What a dumb name, if it's that hard to pro-
nounce!" cry the fake teeth. "So what d'ya want
already, kid?"

"I want to know how to get to Fairyland!"
exclaims Rollo. "I'm on a brave quest to rescue
my mom, so where is it? Fairyland, I mean." (A
hero should always impressively explain what
he's up to, Rollo knows.)

"'Fairyland' . . ." repeat the teeth. "Hoo boy,
that's a tough one."

"But Marv Tweetie said you'd know," insists
Rollo, in dismay.

"Did he now? He said that? Well, we'll have
to think, then. Hoo boy, lemme see."

"Well, what about goblins?" Rollo cries.

"Goblins? Big hairy fellas?"

"No. Little smelly ones! Don't you know
anything! *Where's Fairyland?*"

"Hey, you just watch your tone of voice,
kiddo," snap the teeth. Menacingly. "Just

45

'cause I'm small! You *hear* me?"

"I'm—I'm sorry," gulps Rollo. "I'm just trying, you know, to courageously rescue my mom, and I need directions."

"Yeah? Well, you just mind your manners, Corky Courageous," warn the teeth. "Now I *will* answer your question, okay? But first . . . *first* . . . why, *first* you gotta show me you got the physical fitness to even *handle* a quest."

"You mean demonstrate my samurai stick-fighting technique? Here?" says Rollo, confused.

"Samu-wha? Nah, let's see ya do twenty push-ups. Good ones," the teeth add.

Now of all activities Rollo despises, push-ups rank close to the top.

"Aw, *come on*!" he protests in disbelief.

But it's no use. Shocking as it is to say, brave questing Rollo has to suffer the astounding, trying indignity of getting down on his hands and knees, right there among the bushes and the litter, and doing push-ups for a set of joke dentures. Su-ichi Samurai Swordboy never remotely suffered like this—certainly never for an oracle.

"That's fourteen . . ." say the false teeth,

counting. "Fifteen, but you're cheating. . . ."

Rollo strains, his Jellyfish shirt smudged with dirt; no luck. "I can't do any more," he gasps.

"Well, I guess then I can't help you," announce the false teeth, oh so airily.

At which point Rollo loses his temper and grabs his hockey stick and threatens to bash the oracle to pieces. "Just tell me where's Fairyland!" he snarls.

"Okay, okay," clack the teeth. "Geez, enough with the rough stuff! Fact is, I, personally, do not know where Fairyland is. But I understand Harv does."

"Harv?" says Rollo, baffled. "Who's Harv? You mean *Marv*? But Marv's a goner—his stomach exploded, from overeating waffles." The words sound ludicrous, but also gruesome. Like everything else that's been going on recently in Rollo's world.

"No, Harv, *Harv*," insist the teeth. "Beats me who he is. I'm just a small operation here, kid, what d'ya want, an encyclopedia!"

Rollo sags in confusion.

"Whew," say the false teeth. "Now that's

over, got any gum or candy? I'm starving, I could eat a horse."

But Rollo isn't listening. He's suddenly feeling overwhelmed. Confusion, frustration, desperation: take your pick. None are feelings, honestly, that Rollo's great with. He's just trying to be courageous, and uncravenly, and look what he's had to go through—look where he is now, being ordered around and mystified by a set of fake dentures in the bushes! It's like a nightmare!

Yes, *exactly* like a nightmare.

"Wait a minute," sputters Rollo, as it dawns on him, better late than never.

Maybe he's dreaming again?

But how to tell?

"Ungh! Ungh!" grunts Rollo, desperately pinching himself to see if he can make himself wake up.

"Hey, that sounds like pinching, to me!" yip the false teeth. "I *love* pinching—lemme in there!" And they spring high off their tree stump and fasten onto the flesh of Rollo's nose.

"Ow! Ow!" yelps Rollo.

"Grrr! Grrr!" grunt the savage dentures, gnashing away.

Yelping Rollo drops his samurai stick and hops around, twisting and tugging to pry the teeth off. But they're too strong! Finally with a yell he tears them away, but they seize onto his thumb, like a mad crab. Madly Rollo tries to shake them off, then he just wallops them over and over against the tree stump. With a *sproing!* the false teeth break apart and fall to the ground.

Ferociously Rollo leaps up and down on his white-and-pink former oracle, cursing, with both feet.

"Despicable young brute!"

It's the fat old pigeon lady.

"Those dentures must belong to some poor elderly soul! Craven creep!" She comes charging into the bushes, swinging her shopping bag. Rollo tries to fend her off, but her bag catches him smack in his smarting nose. *"Ow!"* he squawks again. He reels back, and his heel catches on the tree-stump root and he sprawls to the ground. The old lady flops down onto him with her full weight, like she's doing a cannonball at a seniors' swim center.

"Police! Police!" she hollers, as Rollo squirms and thrashes, pinned under her.

"Get off! Get off!" he gasps.

Police whistles shriek. The sounds of footsteps come thundering. Pigeons storm and zoom.

"That's him! The shoplifter!" The scrawny store owner rushes up, panting, his fractured spectacles crudely taped. Two big panting policemen appear beside him.

"No, stop—" sputters Rollo, scarcely able to breathe. "You don't understand—I'm on a—qu—"

and his eyes fly open and he shoves the old lady off.

Only it's not the old lady. It's his pillow.

He gapes at it. He's in his bed. In his bedroom.

Noreen sneers from the doorway. "Why are you *screaming*?" she hisses. "Renee and Mrs. Schnockler—Lola—are downstairs, do you want them to think I've got a *freak* for a brother, why do you always screw everything up?"

"Ungh," blinks Rollo; yet again.

"And weren't you supposedly going to go rescue Mom? Pathetic loser!"

And she slams the door.

Again.

Whoo-hoo!
50
pages!

Seven

In other words, it's all been just another dream? Rollo's still not managed to leave the house?

"Aw, *no*," groans our would-be hero, grimacing at his alarm clock, which says eleven A.M. in its bright little prim way. "This is *terrible*," Rollo adds, to make the point.

He drags himself out of bed and dresses in a huff, sulkily yanking on his Jellyfish jersey. He grabs his backpack and his samurai hockey stick. He stalks out the door—but he doesn't go charging down the stairs. No, he stops; because gales of giggles and clapping sweep up from below. Rollo creeps to the banister, and furtively peers down. Right there in the living room, Noreen and Renee—and yes, Mrs. Schnockler ("Lola")!—are staging a fashion show, featuring Rollo's mom's clothes. And her jewelry, which lies scattered around everywhere, along with all sorts of cosmetics.

The sight makes Rollo's blood boil with outrage. How completely shameless!

No way he's going down to the front door past this scene, to subject himself to their scorn and titters.

He'll sneak out the back way.

Rollo turns, and nips off down the hall, bent double, like Su-ichi Samurai Swordboy sneaking away after spotting Ghost Demon Assassins and Iron Warriors lying in ambush. He reaches the back staircase and starts down; and to his concern, he sees Lola Schnockler's little white toy poodle, Snowflake, at the bottom by the laundry room.

"Snowflake—*ssh*!" he calls out in an urgent whisper, to warn the doggie not to start yapping and give him away.

Snowflake looks up at Rollo from under his

red bow (which he wears even though he's a he). He wags his pom-pommed tail. Then he lifts his leg to pee.

"Snowflake—stop!" Outraged, Rollo thumps down the steps. "Bad dog!" he scolds. *"Bad!"* He threatens Snowflake with his hockey stick, which is not exactly heroic or proper treatment of animals, but is understandable, given the yellow puddle right by the back door.

Snowflake yips and scampers around Rollo and bounds up onto the stairs. Then he turns and yips at Rollo some more, without a trace of guilt.

"Bad Snowflake!" Rollo snarls. *"Bad!"* Snowflake snarls right back. Then he grins, wagging his tail. His little sharp face turns more sharp-nosed; and old, and goblinlike.

"Quit calling me Snowflake," he announces. "I'm Harv."

The words so shock Rollo that he reels back. Understandably. His hockey stick clunks against the wall. He gapes, as he's been doing a lot recently. *"H-Harv?"* he says at last, feeling the dizziest, eeriest twisting of reality. "You mean the Harv wh-who the *oracle* said knows how—how to get to—to *Fairyland*?"

"I'm Harv!" repeats the doggie, merrily. "I'm Harv!" And he rears up on his little hind legs and shuffle dances this way and that on the stair step, like at a talent show. *I'm Harv, I'm Harv, I'm Harv!"* he sings.

The sound of hurrying paws drums from above. Rollo stares up—he gasps. Another little white doggie with a red bow grins down at him from the top of the stairs. It's an exact replica of Snowflake. It barks, merrily.

"I'm Harv!" it announces.

It comes bounding down.

Suddenly a mob of Snowflake replicas comes flooding after it down the staircase.

I'm Harv, I'm Harv, I'm Harv!" they all sing.

"Stop—" sputters Rollo, lurching back against the door. "Stop!" he shouts, as the avalanche of Snowflakes reaches the bottom of the stairs and leaps up into the air, right for his head. He bashes and flails with his hockey stick at the red bows, at the sharp little white snouts, but there are too many—too many snapping, clawing, gouging—

"Stop!" he squawks—

and his eyes fly open, and he batters away the swarm on his head. They clunk against the wall. But they're his backpack.

"Wha—" gulps Rollo.

He's in bed—but not his bed. A narrow, bottom bunk. In a small, dim room. With lots of bars.

Eight

"Hey, shut up!" whines a hard, groggy young voice in the bunk above Rollo. "You woke me up! Weirdo!"

"I was having a dream," mumbles Rollo.

"So what! *Jellyfish jerk.*"

"You're the jerk . . ." Rollo grumbles, and he pulls his precious NuttiNutz-laden backpack to him, which two scary kids with weird, ugly haircuts had tried to wrestle away from him in the big holding pen before he was put in this cell. He pinches himself again, just to be sure; but no use. His nose still hurts too.

Rollo's in jail.

Jail is where they put you when you're
arrested for shoplifting and assaulting two elderly persons.

It didn't matter when he protested that the
"merchandise" was given to him by a stranger
he'd just met—

"Meaning the deceased, Marvin Tweetie?"
interrupted the police gruffly. "Meaning your
accomplice, who ate so many waffles, his stomach actually—actually—" And they tittered, and
then they sputtered, and then they burst out
laughing, repeating *"stomach exploded!"* and
"waffle overdose!" as if it were a big joke. Rollo
tried to grin along with them, even though he
was shocked at their cruelty.

But it didn't matter. No, nor did it matter
that the owner of the magic shop bashed *him*
with his own hockey stick and that the pigeon
lady was squashing *him* to death. Of course,
these last two details didn't reflect well on a
would-be hero, and Rollo went quite red saying
them.

"Yeah yeah, save it for juvenile court," the
police muttered, still chuckling.

So Rollo decided finally to inform them of his mother's kidnapping, and of his "urgent solo mission," for which he'd need his samurai stick back. Whereupon they just looked at each other, and started laughing all over again. Then they told him to make it snappy with his one allowed phone call; which he did, going red faced once more.

But no one answered at home. He left a message.

That was yesterday. Neither his dad nor Noreen have called back all this time—Noreen's probably glad he's behind bars! He can just imagine her gloating.

There now in his narrow harsh bunk, Rollo tries to comfort himself by brooding some more on Su-ichi Samurai Swordboy's ordeal in the dungeons of the Robot Reptiles; but it's gloomy comfort. *"Cravenly cowards,"* he mutters, about his father and sibling. He swallows the remains of the NuttiNutz he started in the dark after the order for "Lights out!" *"Treacherous,"* he adds, touching the Band-Aid on his nose, which is still sore from where the fake dentures attacked him.

"Will ya *shut up* already?" squawks the kid above. He pounds on the side of the bunk.

"Hey, what's the racket!" growls a gruff voice. A guard stands sour and vexed at the cell bars. "It's six o'clock in the morning!" He yawns irritably. His fat cheeks are dark with stubble.

"He keeps yelling, waking me up!" whines the kid in the top bunk.

"I was having a bad dream," Rollo explains. Wishing that's what was going on now.

"Hey, what's the racket!" echoes a second guard, joining the first.

"Hockey nutball," says the fat guard. "Causing a disturbance, claims it's nightmares."

"Oh, punk with the leprechauns, beat up the old folks," sneers the second guard.

"I didn't beat anybody up," protests Rollo. "And they weren't leprechauns—"

His cellmate whines.

"Know what? I think we got ourselves a 'mental,'" declares the second guard. He taps the side of his head.

"Yeah," agrees the first guard. "'Mental,' all the way." He sighs. "Okay, I'll take him up." He brings out his big keys. "Come on, Jellyfish, we're outa here."

"Weirdo," hisses the kid above.

"You mean you're letting me out now?" asks Rollo, in relief, but concern too, as the fat guard huffs along, gripping his arm, steering him slowly up several flights of musty, dreary iron stairs. "'Cause I really need my hockey stick back. It's my samurai swordstick."

The guard smirks. "Nah, we're not letting you out yet, Jellyfish." He pants from the stair climbing. "And I think we'll keep your hockey stick; how many more innocent people you wanna attack?"

"But you don't understand," protests Rollo. "I need to find somebody . . . somebody called . . ." His voice trails off; they plod now down a long bare corridor with mildewed, stony walls, lit only by a few dim, flickering bare lightbulbs.

It's one of the most dismal places Rollo's ever seen.

The guard chuckles. "Don't worry, you can go find whoever you want." He tightens his grip. "Only first you got to spend ten to twenty years in a cold, awful, faraway place, where you can talk all you want about goblins and tooth fairies and the four-leaf clovers with other nutballs just like you. You just tell the doctor *everything*."

"What do you mean? What doctor?" says Rollo. Chill dread closes over him; he hates doctors and dentists.

"You know, the *head* doctor." The guard taps under his hat.

"Wait," protests Rollo, in general.

But they're waiting already, in front of a battered metal door. "Oh, you're gonna love this doctor," the guard whispers. He winks, evilly. He knocks. He opens the door, sticks in his head and bawls, "Another fruitcake for ya, Doc!" And with a yank of Jellyfish shirt he thrusts Rollo inside and slams the door after him.

Rollo stumbles into an office: a dreary, forbidding place with tall metal cabinets and peculiar sinister contraptions with lots of leather straps. A thin man in a stained white coat stands beside a metal desk. He stares out the window, his back to Rollo.

"So what's your name, you sick, *evil* boy . . ." he sighs.

His voice is strangely familiar.

"R-Rollo. B-but I—"

"Raleigh?" repeats the doctor, irritably. He peers around.

Rollo gasps. The doctor has a long, drooping moustache, and an eye patch—only now covering the other eye.

"Marv Tweetie!" blurts Rollo, in shock.

The doctor glares at him. "Not *Marv*," he snarls. "What a ridiculous mistake, Marv's my twin brother! I'm *Harv*," he exclaims. And he stamps his foot. "I'm *Harvey* Tweetie!"

Nine

The obvious question you'd expect from Rollo, at this point, under these astounding circumstances, would be, in a staggered voice:

"The Harv, or H-Harvey, who knows how to get to F-Fairyland?"

And that is exactly what Rollo comes out with, his grin of delight growing wider and wilder, to match his eyes.

At which the white-coated doctor flinches back, almost shrinking against the window. "Who said?" he demands. He darts a one-eyed look this way and that. *"Marv said that?"*

"Well, not Marv, I mean—not really—" cries

Rollo; and then he hesitates, because he's unsure if he should mention Marv Tweetie's terrible end: because what if Harv Tweetie doesn't know yet? "It was an oracle—kind of," he just says finally; and he snorts. "These stupid fake false teeth."

At which Harv Tweetie peers at him. "Why 'stupid'?" he says.

"Yeah," pipes another voice in the room. A familiar voice. *Why 'stupid'?"*

Rollo swings around; to his further shock he sees, right there in a bookshelf, whole as can be, the joke dentures themselves!

"But didn't—but I just smashed you to bits!" he protests in confusion. "In the park. After you *attacked* me."

"Never laid eyes on you in my life," the teeth reply, sniffily, so to speak.

"You're *lying*!" sputters Rollo. His head spins from so many strange bafflements. But his freshly throbbing nose—that's certain, indisputable. "Marv Tweetie gave you to me," he snarls, his hands gripping for his absent hockey stick. "From the magic shop!"

"You calling somebody a liar, bucky boy?"

snarl back the teeth. They clatter with menace.
"Eh? Eh?"

"Manners, manners, you two!" exclaims
Harv Tweetie. "Maybe it was one of your
brethren at the store, Mo."

"Maybe . . ." allow the false teeth, grudgingly.
"Maybe. In which case, if it was Joe"—there's a
snort—"stupid would be right!"

"Joe?" says Rollo.

"Just like Marv, to copy what I do!" exclaims
Harv Tweetie, pounding his white-coated thigh
and ignoring Rollo. "I'm the one who had joke
dentures as a pal first! I'm the one!" And he stamps
his foot again. "So how d'you know Marv? He
start you on your life of crime? Where is he?"

"I—Marv—" Rollo gulps. Then desperately
he just blurts out the awful waffle-related news.

At which Harv Tweetie flinches again, and
shudders. "The Curse of the Tweeties!" he cries in
a stricken voice. "We're too nutty about sweets!"
He twists around and snatches something from a
small plastic tub on the desk—a stick of celery. He
snaps off a crunching bite. "Tell me," he demands,
his eye patch heaving and his moustache twitching

as he chews. "Was it a really, *really* painful death? Did he suffer, *terribly*?"

Rollo gulps once more, remembering the gruesome gasping figure in the diner booth. "Pr-probably."

Harv Tweetie swallows. *"Good,"* he grins. "At least that's *some* consolation!"

And he sniggers, in savage satisfaction.

Rollo stares at him, shocked. Suddenly, despite himself, he sniggers too. Then suddenly he bursts out laughing. "Yeah," he hoots giddily, "it was kinda *sickening!*"

And the dreary scary office rocks with their cruel laughter, all three of them, Rollo and Harv Tweetie and the joke dentures named Mo.

"So please, *please*, you gotta tell me how to get to Fairyland," Rollo cries. "And please let me go!"

At which Harv Tweetie abruptly stops laughing.

"I'm not crazy or anything," Rollo insists. "I'm on a noble quest, see, to rescue—"

"Noble quest, listen to him!" mock the teeth. "Crazy, this isn't?"

"No, I'm not!—I mean, yes, I am," retorts

Rollo, trying to reply to both parts of these outrageous remarks, and getting tangled. Really, the false teeth are as obnoxious as his sister! For the umpteenth time he desperately relates what happened at Pleasant Lake, and the cravenly cowardice of his other family members about a mission to Fairyland.

"Fairyland . . . !" Harv Tweetie cries out the word in a whisper. He stares off one–eyed into space. Then he wrenches away. He stalks over toward the metal cabinets. He stops. He twists this way and that, as if struggling, his bony hands clenched. It's truly a sight. "I'm done with Fairyland," he squawks, in a strangled voice. "Fairyland, it's in the past! And it's too danger-ous. In a personal way . . ."

"Then just tell me, and I'll go!" cries out Rollo, a chill of excitement sweeping over him at the atmospherics of the scene.

"Pushy, pushy," clack the teeth.

Harv Tweetie flaps his hand dismissively. "You'll never find Fairyland by yourself. And if you did, you'll never find where the goblins hang out!"

"Then you must come with, and show me!" insists Rollo wildly. "Just like the old blind Dragon Scout who went along with—"

"Pushy!" repeat the teeth.

"I'm not being *pushy*!" snarls Rollo.

"'*Come with*' you?" repeats Harv Tweetie—as if the words were incomprehensible. He laughs, in scorn. And then he stops. And then he wrenches this way and that again, clenching his skinny fists, consumed in a desperate inner struggle of some kind. Really, if you like melodrama, he's your guy, and how.

"*All right*—" he gasps suddenly. And he twists about to face Rollo, but staring into space above Rollo's head. "Why *not*, eh?" He gives a wild laugh. "Oh, I'm sick o' this charade, wasting away here ministering to a lot of wretched little psychos like you—okay, not like you. But I'm Harv Tweetie—an adventurer at heart! A *real* adventurer, not like that *wannabe*, Marv!"

And with these words of scorn for his dead twin he tears off his stained white coat, revealing a stained safari jacket, like what big game hunters wear and get food stains on.

"This time I *will* bring back a goblin alive!" he cries out. "Though they do stink when they get excited! But never mind—and never mind about the goblin treasure." He gulps. "Nor the Curse of the Tweeties."

"What 'goblin treasure'?" asks Rollo, wide-eyed, as Harv Tweetie stalks past across the room.

"Never mind," mutters the adventurer mysteriously. He's a big one for teases, too.

He wrestles open a metal cabinet. "But let's make haste, make haste if we're going. And not out the front door, no no, too obvious. *Out the fireplace chimney*," he declares, grinning craftily.

"What fireplace chimney?" says Rollo, not having noticed one at all. "'Cause first—"

"That one," snaps Harv Tweetie. Then he looks confused. Suddenly he laughs—a strained laugh. "Fooled you!" he gulps. "There isn't any."

"Gotcha, dumbo!" jeer the false teeth.

"Out the window, out the window!" cries Harv Tweetie. And he claps on his head an old-fashioned explorer's helmet that's so large it comes down almost past his nose, and drags out a bundled rope ladder, and starts hauling it across the floor.

"But wait," cries Rollo, even as, elated, he jumps over to help. "They took my hockey stick, it's my samurai swordstick, I need it back!"

"Over there . . . in the corner," pants Harv Tweetie, as they wrestle the rope ladder up onto the windowsill. "I had it sent along, to sell back to you. I'll give you a good price: $2000? No? Okay, $10.99?"

"But it's *my* hockey stick," protests Rollo, running over to it.

"Oh, all right, you can owe me," grumbles Harv Tweetie. He feeds the ladder out the window. "One would think that out of appreci—" He stares suddenly toward the door. *"Hello?"* he calls. "Who is it?" There's silence. "Quick, they may be on to us!" And he disappears over the windowsill with the false teeth perched on his shoulder, like a parrot.

Rollo rushes back from the corner and peers out after him. "C-c-o-ol!" he gulps, the wind whipping up his hair. It's a long, long way down to a tiny stony prison courtyard, along a thin rope ladder that twists and squirms as Harv Tweetie and his shoulder passenger shrink away in descent. At this point Rollo notices a fire escape right beside the window and wonders why they don't just—

"Too obvious!" comes back Harv's faint cry. *"Hurry up!"*

So, with his heart in his mouth, Rollo dutifully clambers over, and starts down. The wind whistles, the ladder twists and sways—hard as he can Rollo thinks of Su-ichi Samurai Swordboy's perilous escape from the tower of the Zombie Crow King. Downward he inches, rung by rung, poking about shakily with a sneaker toe for each next shifting foothold. Best not to look below anymore, he's decided. Not that he's afraid of heights, well, okay, a bit. But who wouldn't be now, clinging to a pair of scrawny ropes ninety feet in midair outside a prison tower! And the ladder keeps sort of twirling alarmingly, perhaps because Rollo's gripping it so tight. And because the wind keeps gusting.

"Jeepers . . ." Rollo murmurs.

Despite himself he sneaks a gulping peek

down—and he gasps, because the courtyard is still so far below. Whereupon cooing erupts in his ears—wings flurry into him.

Pigeons!

"Beat it—" Rollo squawks. He lashes out frantically with his hockey stick. The rope ladder lurches. He flails again as the pigeons swarm, acting like they're all Zombie Crow wannabes. The rope ladder veers stupendously.

And just like that Rollo and his backpack go swinging across the tower, from one side to the other, in the manner of a human pendulum.

"Whoa-oa-oa!" gasps Rollo, sweeping and twirling over to the right, birds in pursuit.

"Whoa-oa-oa!" again, twirling and sweeping back over to the left, birds in reverse pursuit.

It's like a daredevil circus act, like an astoundingly reckless carnival ride. It's not what Rollo had in mind in the least. Complicated further by him trying to fend off pigeons while hanging on for dear life, in fear of the rope ladder coming untied.

And you know what pigeons like to do.

"Don't—" Rollo squawks, cringing as the

angry pests squirt at him, their messes just missing, splatting against the tower.

"*Help!*" he cries, or whisper-cries, bravely not wanting to draw attention from inside the prison. "*Help!*"

But there's no help in midair, not from the courtyard below or anywhere else.

In desperation Rollo lunges for the tower wall, to try to slow himself down. His shoulder rams into rough stone, he bounces wildly straight off—"Ow!"—and for a terrifying moment, loses his grip on the ropes. Then loses his hockey stick as he grabs half back on. The hockey stick plummets out of sight.

Downward Rollo flounders, fast and then faster—too fast, with burning hands he's hurtling down, down— "*O-o-o-o-h!*"—right down *smash* onto some plastic garbage cans. The rope ladder comes tumbling down on top of him in a writhing heap. Which receives a *splat* of good riddance from the pigeons.

"*Quiet!*" snarl the fake teeth.

That's the sum total of concern they show for Rollo's well-being after his hair-raising descent.

He's alive, somehow, no thanks to anyone else; shaken to the core, but uninjured, miraculously.

"And watch it with the hockey stick," add the teeth, *"ya almost hit me!"*

"Ungh," groans Rollo; as he seems to have been doing much of recently.

Harv Tweetie crouches by the foot of the tower this whole time, moodily crunching on a carrot stick from one of his elaborate pockets. He stares dismally under his helmet past the garbage cans at the big door across the courtyard.

"I left the key back upstairs . . ." he announces.

So much for the first part of their brilliant escape.

After a pause, Rollo groggily clears his head enough to suggest, very unenthusiastically, going back up the fire escape. "Too obvious," he's told. And the rope ladder of course is on the ground. But what about the courtyard door, are they sure— "'Course it's locked!" he's informed, with a snort, by the joke dentures. "This is a prison, bub."

"Stymied," mutters Harv Tweetie. "We'll just

have to wait till someone enters, and brazen our way out. But how'd the rope ladder get so messy?" he demands irritably. "That's prison property!"

Incredibly, or maybe not so incredibly, two full hours go by. No one enters. So no *crafty* escape still. This sort of thing happens often with clever plans, alas.

"Well, guess I'll just have to get someone to come down, and open up," sighs Harv Tweetie, grimly.

And to Rollo's disbelief he steps out into full view, and begins shouting and waving his arms and jumping and screaming. A few heads glance down from barred windows in the high court-yard walls. Shoulders shrug; they move on. That's it.

"Incredible!" mutters Harv Tweetie.

He puts two fingers in under his moustache and blasts a shrieking whistle that ricochets spectacularly off the surrounding walls.

In reply: silence.

"Stymied!" curses Harv Tweetie.

Which is not what you want to hear a lot from your guide.

At this point Rollo takes matters into his own sore hands, and scurries stiffly across the courtyard with his hockey stick and just starts bashing in fury at the big door, as if it were pigeons and goblins and false teeth all rolled into one.

"Stop, stop, are you *mad*?" cries Harv Tweetie. "Do you want to give us away?"

"Psycho, psycho, told you, told you," chant the false teeth.

Naturally the door doesn't move. Rollo turns sheepishly panting to the onrushing ex-doctor and dental work. Whereupon, with a slow creak behind him, the door very slowly . . . swings *inward* . . . wide open.

A dirtied little cat stands peering up at the gaping man and boy. *"Miaaow?"* it says.

"Nice kitty," declares Harv Tweetie, swallowing, with an uncertain attempt at a grin. He cautiously reaches out a hand. The cat growls.

"Heads up!" blurt the teeth.

Harv Tweetie shrinks back. The cat hisses. Rollo also shrinks back.

"N-nice kitty!" plead all three voices.

The cat hisses again and takes a step. With a courageous cry, Rollo pokes at it with his samurai swordstick. The cat squeals and batters with its claws—then rockets away out of sight.

The would-be escapees stare.

"Vanquished!" Harv Tweetie cries gleefully.

Out the empty doorway they all clatter, to freedom.

"Man, were you scared of that cat!" the teeth sneer back at Rollo, not showing the least appreciation.

"Not as much as *you* were!" Rollo sneers back.

And on this note Rollo finally gets under way—on the route to Fairyland.

"So where is it?" he calls breathlessly, huffing along under the barbed wire–topped prison walls behind the bobbing explorer helmet of Harv Tweetie.

"Where is what?" Harv Tweetie calls back.

Where is what?

neT

Huh?

"Wh-what d'you mean, 'Where is what?'" pants Rollo, in confusion, not to say alarm, there in mid–jail break—scuttling down the deserted little street that runs along the grim granite prison walls.

The galloping adventurer glances back. He's grinning. He winks. *"Just joshing!"*

"Gotcha!" chime the teeth. "Gotcha *mucho*!" And they guffaw, but in such an aggressive, mean-spirited way that much of the shared fun that could be in the joke is lost.

All this yucking however causes the fake

dentures to lose their grip on Harv Tweetie's jacket shoulder. Off they tumble, squawking, and bounce onto the ground.

Now it's Rollo's turn to laugh aggressively. Which he does, stopping and clutching his belly in exaggerated mirth. "Ha ha ha!" he guffaws, pointing.

"Shut up! Shut up!" gnash the joke dentures, spitting dirt.

This is not the sort of scene you might expect in a noble quest, but there it is.

"Stop!" squawks Harv Tweetie, in a hushed voice. He's stopped himself, in the midst of reaching down for his fallen passenger.

He stares back past Rollo with a piercing grim single eye.

"Got the old chill . . ." he murmurs. "Someone . . . *or something* . . . is following us."

Rollo edges around. "Who?"

But there's no one in sight: only the vast granite slabs of the prison . . . and the empty, dusty street they've been running down. . . . And eerie silence. . . .

"Away, away!" cries Harv Tweetie's voice, his bootsteps clattering off again.

"Wait!" shouts Rollo. He chases after. "But you didn't answer. Where is it—*Fairyland, I mean*?"

"Not so *loud*!" Harv Tweetie hisses back, glaring around one eyed under his low helmet. "The walls have ears!"

"Wouldn't you like to know," taunt the joke dentures, back on their perch.

And like this the three escapees go racing away from the long, gloomy shadows of the high prison walls.

But really: where *is* Fairyland?

Eleven

"Pleasant Lake? Spare me, oh, *please*. . . ."

"Yeah, we were just there, *imagine*?" yawns Noreen, phonily blasé, as if she was entirely bored by Renee's generalized snicker about the place.

The topic has somehow come up while they're on a break from flirting at the mall, where their new borrowed jewelry accessories have provoked interest and, better yet, shock and envy. "*Pleasant Lake*, it's so *nowhere*, nothing *ever* happens there," drawls Noreen. "It's so like—for *losers*."

And she rolls her heavily cosmeticized eyes.

* * *

"Pleasant Lake," Rollo murmurs to himself. Blinking in puzzlement.

But that's where he's headed now—hurtling along on his quest in Harv Tweetie's car, which was parked way off in an abandoned lot, to save on prison parking fees. Except the lot turned out not to be abandoned. And guess who wound up paying the grinning owner?

And Harv Tweetie's car is so ancient, it could come from an antique car museum. Except it doesn't look like it's ever been washed, and its wheels are crooked, and its tires are almost flat, and its doors are scraped and dented, and its bumpers sag, and its muffler obviously has a hole, and black smoke squirts and billows from its backfiring exhaust. "PRISON AMBULANCE— PRIVATE" is painted somewhat confusingly on its hood and sides. It resembles very little the rainbow-powered eagle chariot, which the Wind Gods loaned Su-ichi Samurai Swordboy on his journey to the stronghold of the Robot Reptiles.

"But if Fairyland is by Pleasant Lake, like you say," mutters Rollo, still perplexed by Harv

Tweetie's dramatic announcement of where they were off to, "how come we never *heard* about it?" A certain person's voice echoes sneering in his head. He bounces in his seat, Harv Tweetie being an alarmingly bad driver.

The adventurer's good eye twitches irritably, taking itself off the road again. The dashing stained white scarf he now sports flaps and whirls dangerously around his helmet in the window breeze. "Don't you ever *listen*, Raleigh?" he snaps. "Are you *so* far gone in depraved criminal psychohood, you can't *heed*?"

His tone displays a similar exasperation to the one Rollo's dad gets with him, except Harv Tweetie's involves the crunching and spraying of celery and carrot too. As with the other twin, Rollo does a lot of brushing off of his Jellyfish shirt.

"It's *Rollo*," Rollo corrects stubbornly. "It's just that Noreen—"

His words are drowned out by the blare of the antique rubber-bulb car horn that Harv Tweetie blasts at a bicyclist, who looks around wildly and careens off the road, and crashes somersaulting into the trees.

"Not any old '*by Pleasant Lake*'—know what to *look* for, *do you? Eh?*" demands Harv Tweetie, continuing. "And *comprehend* what you're seeing? Can't simply *use* the map!" he snorts. He raps at his elaborate safari pocket containing an honest-to-God special map of Fairyland. "Got to *decipher* it. *Crafty*, understand? That's what it takes, I keep telling you: *crafty! Eh*, Mo?" he says, to the false teeth on their seat on the dashboard.

"*Crafty,*" reply the joke dentures.

But it's this *crafty* mumbo jumbo that's put Harv Tweetie in such a foul mood. It was his *crafty* idea to take a long, devious route to Pleasant Lake, in case someone *or something* might be in pursuit—a fine idea maybe, only they've gotten lost at least four times. Now it's hours since they started out, the end of the afternoon as they finally blast past a sign stating "Pleasant Lake – Picnic Paradise – 5 Miles."

"You couldn't even spell *crafty*, Jellybean—*Jellybeanieweenie,*" sneer the false teeth at Rollo, bouncing on their perch.

That's how they've been the whole trip: as insufferably rude as Noreen. They've made several more ultrasnarky references to Rollo's quest. Troublingly, when Rollo ignored them and switched to the topic of samurais and such with Harv Tweetie, the adventurer not only knew as little as his deceased twin—he seemed almost, well, *scornful*. And he just grunted on the topic of amazing, weird dreams. And only muttered, "Don't tell me about 'em," regarding older sisters. . . . So it hasn't been a complete social pleasure, this ride, despite its goal. Not like the good fellowship always on display in the adventures of the Samurai Swordboy—not by a long shot.

"'Course I can spell '*crafty*'!" Rollo informs the insulting teeth. His hands grip his hockey stick, there between his legs, in case anybody gets notions of nose-jumping. "And quit insulting the Jellyfish," he demands, preparing to tell a lie, "'cause they were the *awesomest* team *ever*—so . . . so double *beanieweenies* to *you*!"

"Hoo, listen to him!" hoot the teeth. "Everybody knows they were *stinko*! *Jellybeanieweenie, Jellybeanieweenie!*"

This interesting sports discussion is interrupted by another stunning blast of Harv Tweetie's horn.

The car swerves violently—barely missing two bicyclists who've already crashed and were standing in the road clutching a broken arm each and then waving desperately with their good arms at the oncoming PRISON AMBULANCE–PRIVATE— before diving for their lives.

The swerving causes the joke dentures to rocket back and forth yelping across the dashboard. At which Rollo brays with exaggerated laughter as he jars against the door. For a second he thinks of rolling down his window all the way, so the teeth might go shooting out, with a little help.

But he restrains himself.

Harv Tweetie curses back down the road, shaking his bony fist. The ancient car thunders on, skidding around a bend, and then on around the next, on toward Fairyland, supposedly. Then suddenly it slows down. It stops. It sits, rumbling and backfiring. The adventurer peers around intently over his shoulder, which is crowded with scarf.

"What is it?" says Rollo.

"Ecch, I feel *dizzy* . . ." grumble the false teeth.

"Got the old chill," mutters Harv Tweetie grimly. "Someone, *or something,* is following us. . . . But why's everything *white*?"

"It's your *scarf*," Rollo informs him, stunned at the obvious. Then he stares back himself: and sees only the long, empty road, curving away under the tall pines in the dimming sunlight. In eerie silence.

"Hmm . . ." murmurs Harv Tweetie, view now clear. Uneasily he turns away. "We must hurry!" And the ancient car roars, and lurches off.

"*Ech-ch-ch* . . ." splutter the joke dentures.

"Somebody's carsick," chants Rollo, in delight.

The joke dentures try to reply, but just burp sickishly instead.

In this way, at last, right as the sun is setting, the vehicle of Rollo's quest pulls in clanking and clunking and blasting and smoke belching to the empty picnic area at Pleasant Lake.

Without waiting politely to help unload, Rollo jumps out and rushes to the picnic table where the terrible events occurred—just about at this very time of day. He gulps, seeing some plates from their supper still in the grass by a bench.

"Mom?" he calls out, wildly. His heart pounds as he scans around, samurai swordstick at the ready. *So where is it, then—Fairyland?*

Beyond, ghostly dark and glimmering at its edges, Pleasant Lake spreads wide, catching the final faint gloss of twilight. Early fireflies wink.

But Rollo on his noble quest isn't looking at any of this.

"H-hey!" he stammers. He blinks. "Hey!" he shouts. Wildly again.

He rushes off toward one end of a small stand of trees—where a sign stuck in the ground announces, "**FAIRYLAND! THIS WAY!**" Just like that: with a rim of little electric bulbs blinking around it, and a big angled arrow pointing down.

"But how—how could we have missed it?" exclaims Rollo, coming up.

"No, stop—wait!" cries Harv Tweetie, from the finally opened trunk of the car.

Grinning in disbelief, Rollo gapes down mesmerized at what's under the arrow.

A set of curiously crude, peculiar-looking steps lead down deep, deep into the ground!

"Cool," Rollo gulps—even daring a quickie furtive pinch of himself, just to check, after a rapid glance to make sure the false teeth aren't nearby yet. But it's no dream: after the pinch, the steps are still there.

"Kinda weird," gulps Rollo some more; and he think how this will shut up his older sister's slanderous face for the rest of her life, and he adds, *"But so-o co-o-ol!"*

And then he turns, because Harv Tweetie doesn't exactly seem to share his delight, he comes charging across from the car, his white scarf flopping. "Heedless young sicko, don't! Don't!" he squawks, waving desperately.

And then he stops, right in his tracks. Slowly he revolves his helmeted head, and peers, toward the other end of the trees. "The old chill?" pipe the false teeth, back on their perch and recovered.

"Got the old chill," announces Harv Tweetie

in his specialty hushed voice. "Someone *or something* is—"

"*Hands up, jerks!*" snarls a voice, interrupting.

An oddly familiar voice.

And someone steps out of the dark trees. With what looks like a great big gun in his hand.

Twelve

Yes: what looks *exactly* like a great big gun.

"*You—*" gasp the ambushed threesome by the Fairyland sign.

"*Officer Ronizoni!*" adds Harv Tweetie. "But how'd you—"

"I said get those hands up!" snarls the fat prison guard, the one with the dark cheeks. "Lift 'em, I say!" He tramps over, wheezing. His cheeks are now shiny with perspiration even in the dimness; his guard uniform is covered with burrs and leafy bits, like you'd get from sneaking hurriedly and clumsily through the woods. "*Surprised*, Doc?" he says, with a taunting chuckle. His eyes glitter loonily. "Whaddya think keyholes are for in office doors?"

"I knew it!" cries Harv Tweetie, hands on high.

"But that's *sneaky*!" protests Rollo. Not that he doesn't eavesdrop himself sometimes, of course, but you always protest when you hear about someone else doing it.

"Shut up, you—Jellyfish *goofball*," the guard snaps back. "*And drop the hockey stick*. No old folks around to attack."

"They attacked *me*," Rollo exclaims, grudgingly doing what he's told. "And that's my *samurai swordstick*, I need it for—"

"*Jellybeanieweenie!*" heckle the false teeth.

"Cut it *out*," snarls Rollo.

"Shut up, both of you!" snarls the guard.

"Now see here," declares Harv Tweetie, "this sick, *evil* boy is under my care—"

"Shut up, shut up—*all of you*!" squawks the guard, his nerves obviously fraying, his cheeks bathed with sweat. He shakes the gun at the three of them. He laughs, wildly. "So I just wanna thank you for leading me right to the entrance to Fairyland. Never knew how to find

it. But from here on"—and he cackles happily—
"I'll just use my map!"

Rollo gawks, stunned. The guard is actually
interested in Fairyland, as opposed to hauling
them back to jail? And he has a map he now
waves about? Which looks exactly like Harv
Tweetie's map of Fairyland, from Rollo's briefly
permitted glimpse of that! "You mean—you
mean there's more than one map?" Rollo sputters to his supposed guide, him and his unique
specialized knowledge.

"'Course there is," snorts the guard.

"Weeniebeanie," murmur the fake dentures.

"*Quit* it!" hisses Rollo.

"You got one free last year when you bought
a jumbo giant pack of NuttiNutz Bars," says the
guard. "And I *lo-ove* NuttiNutz, who doesn't?"

"Yum, yum," say the false teeth. "Got any?"

"My mom wouldn't let me buy a jumbo
giant pack!" recalls Rollo, now with double
regret. He resists the consolation of at least
crowing about what's in his backpack, not wanting it snatched and devoured. Nor even shared,
considering the company.

"I *used* to love 'em all," gulps Harv Tweetie. And he flinches, and then shudders so his arms sway. "NuttiNutz Bars, Cremo-Crud Bars, Sludgie Fudge Pies—toffee and taffy and BananaBomb Fun Flakes! But *now* I love *celery*, and *carrots*!" he insists, his voice straining from his inner turmoil. "But—but you'll never be able to *decipher* the map!"

"Says you," sneers the guard. "Just you watch me, Doc!" And he chuckles, defiantly. He's clearly one of those people who's big on chuckling.

"So *tell* me," he says suddenly, his voice dropping. He steps close, waggling the gun. "So what *is* the goblin treasure?" His eyes are big and eager, like a big kid's. "Is it gold? Silver? *Lotsa shiny jewels*?"

"*Never mind,*" retorts Harv Tweetie, lifting his moustache and chin in the air. "And I don't care how many holes you plug me with."

"Never mind yourself," the prison guard sniffs and steps back. "And so what, too. So long as it's *treasure*. Cause wanna know why I want it? Wanna?"

"No," three voices inform him.

"And you'll probably screw everything up for rescuing my mom!"

"I'm gonna take all that treasure, *whatever* it is," continues Officer Ronizoni, "and get lotsa money for it, and I'm gonna to buy my own theater—and go onstage every night and *yodel*! And everyone in the world will recognize what a great talent I am—*'specially my older sister, Lola!* I, Officer Ronizoni," he cries, "the Yodeling Prison Guard!"

Rollo reels, stupefied again. "You? *You* can't be Lola Schnockler's *brother*!" he sputters, making the wildest of connections as befits all that's transpired.

The prison guard's head snaps around. He looks shocked. "How d'you know her?" He gulps. "What'd she say about my yodeling? She's *lying—what does she know?* She's only a year older! *Keep your arms up!*"

"But she's blond!"

"It's dyed," replies the prison guard. "I've got a *spectacular* yodel—just listen!"

And right there in his guard uniform and hat, with fireflies glimmering around, he steps back another step, and sets himself, and flings up the hand with the map, and bursts out yodeling:

"*Yo do layee, Yo do layee,*" he bellows, in that goofy yodeling style, his neck swelling with effort. "*Yo do layee-ee-ee-ee-ee, Yo do lo!* Good, huh?" he cries.

"Not really . . ." he's informed by the audience, a "tough" audience, to be sure, even with hands in the air.

"You call that yodeling?" add the false teeth, cruelly.

"I had a dream where your sister's *dog* sounded better!" says Rollo, even more cruelly, despite the fact that the prison guard is obviously an oppressed younger brother too.

"So thanks for the lead to Fairyland!" exclaims the yodeler, ignoring the criticism, even chuckling to pretend it had no effect on him, though like any artist, of course, he must be extremely sensitive. "This is where we say 'I'll see ya!'" He tramps forward to the Fairyland sign. "Pretty, pretty," he declares, admiring the peculiar steps there in the ground.

"I wouldn't go down there if I were you," Harv Tweetie informs him.

"Oh you wouldn't," grins Officer Ronizoni, baring his teeth.

"And it's not *fair*, I'm the one on a *quest*!" Rollo protests. Desperately he glances down at his samurai swordstick, lying there uselessly.

"You know, you're all *so rude*," the prison guard announces, twitching, his grin turning really evil, "I'm just gonna have to plug the lot of ya. *What d'ya say to that?*" And with a crazy resentful cackle, he raises his big gun—

"Don't—" squawk the cringing threesome—

And squeezes the trigger.

It crumbles off.

"Drats," he snarls, "I took the one carved out of soap—" He flings it aside with a foamy hand. "Never mind!" he cries, whipping out a spray can from his belt and keeping Rollo and Harv Tweetie at bay with it. "Now don't you come after me or I'll spray you with so much pepper gas you'll choke and go blind!" He gives a little squirt, cackling. Rollo and the adventurer shout and flounder back, covering their faces with their arms.

"Layee-ee-ee-ee-ee, Yo do lo!" yodels the fat, gleeful prison guard, and he jumps down heavily onto the Fairyland steps. Where he lurches, violently, to the sound of splintering and cracking. "Hey—" he gulps.

And he then plunges from sight, as if through a trapdoor, screaming.

Thirteen

Talk about harsh musical criticism!

Rollo scrambles forward, flapping away the pepper spray fumes to snatch up his samurai swordstick. But it's not pepper spray.

"It's air freshener!" cries Rollo. *"Yuck!"*

Swordstick at the ready, the fireflies winking about, he peers down, grimacing and coughing, at where the steps used to be. Now there's only a dark gaping hole, a yard across—its edges jagged with remnants of thin plywood . . . *plywood painted with the 3-D image of steps*!

"Jeepers."

The screams of Officer Ronizoni sink away

farther and farther below, as if from down an immense drainpipe. Which smells like the bathroom in Rollo's house, thanks to the air freshener.

"Goblin booby chute," declares Harv Tweetie, grimly crunching celery beside Rollo while the false teeth finish coughing. "Built to discourage visitors, no fooling. From here on, the countryside's infested with 'em. Imagine a disguised network," he exclaims, "of immense precision-curved tubes, all hundreds and hundreds of yards long and sort of **U**-shaped and interconnected."

"Down one you rocket!" pipe the joke dentures.

"Down one you rocket," continues Harv Tweetie, "then shoot back out its other end, up into the air far away somewhere—but *straight up*, see? And so down you plunge again, *right back in*—rocketing down a different tube now, all over again! You're caught, trapped, never ending! 'Cause each tube's linked with another at each end! Like a chain, *disguised and diabolical*!"

And he shudders.

"You mean this hole is actually the mouth of *more than one* booby chute?" says Rollo, peering.

"Wanna find out?" quip the false teeth. They speak closemouthed now because they're clenched tight to Harv Tweetie's jacket collar, so as not to topple in.

"See *now* why I warned you to keep away," smiles the adventurer. He smirks a little because of how *crafty* he is. "You and that deranged yodel-nut Officer Ronizoni."

To which Rollo can only murmur again the other of his favorite words beside "cool" (it's "jeepers"). He raises his head and gazes out at the darkened landscape. Underneath it, apparently, the Yodeling Prison Guard is rocketing along this very moment! Before shooting back out, somewhere—only to go plunging back in again! Nonstop, like a monstrous version of the waterslides at Roaring Rainbows theme park.

Or like the tunnel traps that the Robot Reptiles dug to guard the entrance to the Abyss fortress in *Su-ichi Samurai Swordboy*!

"*Co-o-ol,*" murmurs Rollo now, naturally. And then a very uncool thought pops into his head. "Hey, wait. If—if the goblin booby chutes are *disguised* . . . how can we always tell to avoid them?"

Which is a truly alarming concern.

"Wouldn't you like to know," snigger the teeth.

"Mind your step," answers Harv Tweetie. "And heed me *always*. 'Cause I know how Fairyland *works*—how to *decipher* the map." He pats the safari jacket pocket in question.

"And now," he announces, very impressive and guidelike, "now there should be a *True Sign* for us . . . *somewhere*."

And sternly, there by the dreadful booby chute, he scans the dark trees and the picnic area with his single piercing eye, for the True Sign.

With a gulp, clutching his samurai sword-stick, Rollo stares around too. And he blinks. "Hey . . ." he says.

Just five yards away, a cloud of fireflies have formed a shaky arrow. Before Rollo's amazed eyes, the words "TRUE SIGN" wobble into winking shape. "Hey, *look!*" cries Rollo, spellbound.

Harv Tweetie's helmet swings about. "Look *where?*" He stares in the wrong direction.

"There! The True Sign, *over there!*" Rollo exclaims frantically. He tugs at the safari jacket.

Really, for a guide with certain kinds of tremendous knowledge, Harv Tweetie has big problems with basics.

"Omigod!" sputters the adventurer, finally getting the picture, his good eye widening. "Whoopi doo, that's it, that's it! Hurry! Hurry!" And he heaves about, this way then that, and barges straight into Rollo, knocking him to the side.

The booby chute side.

And just like that Rollo's foot lurches back onto the jagged very edge of the gaping hole Officer Ronizoni plunged down. "Help!" squawks Rollo, windmilling and flailing, in panic.

So is this how Rollo comes to end up shot out sprawling into the branches of a big dark tree, who knows where in the night?

fourteen

Nope.

Because wrenching about, Rollo just manages to flounder off to the ground, inches away from the booby chute. Where he sprawls, gasping.

"Mind your step, *didn't I warn you*?" Harv Tweetie lectures back, on his way imperviously to the car. "And for God's sake hurry, help with the luggage, you spoiled heedless brat! Or we'll lose the sign!"

"Mind your step, mind your step!" taunt the teeth.

"I *did* mind my step!" snarls Rollo furiously, at the both of them. He's still slapping grassy bits off his Jellyfish uniform shirt as he finally reaches the car. His heart's still racing from the fright he got. "Didn't you *see* what—"

"Coming!" interrupts Harv Tweetie, shouting out to the impatient fireflies, who have switched to spelling out, "LET'S GO ALREADY." Without warning he slams a bag of equipment, splendid with straps, right into Rollo's chest.

"But how do they do that?" pants Rollo. His perfectly legitimate annoyance gives way to awe, as now he lumbers along as fast as he can with his burden (bag of equipment, backpack, hockey stick) beside Harv Tweetie. The fireflies are leading them away.

"That's why they call it Fairyland," grins the eye-patched explorer, huffing from effort. He has the other strap-happy bag of equipment, and a pole with a net at the end for goblin catching.

"It's, you know, what they call 'magic,' *beaniebrain*," pipe the joke dentures from their shoulder perch.

Up past the trees the fireflies lead, away from the picnic area, and then down along a wide slope right below. A big pale moon has risen

straight ahead, and the stars twinkle as if straining their muscles in the evening sky. All of
which makes the dark waters of Pleasant Lake
magically glint and shimmer as it spreads below.
"Shut up," breathes wonderstruck Rollo. Not
every inch of the lake, he notices though, is
glinting and shimmering. One particular spot,
out near the middle, seems to be rumbling . . .
and then boiling. Suddenly, it *explodes*—

and the fat figure of the prison guard bursts
up into the moonlight. He flails in midair, his
screams carrying faintly across the water. And
then he plunges back down into the lake, and
disappears on his next ride.

"Subaquatic booby chute!" exclaims Harv
Tweetie, stopped and gazing in admiration.
"Ingenious valve engineering—keeps it good
and tight."

"Yo do layee-ee-ee-ee-ee!" yodel the false teeth,
meanly.

"Yo do layee-ee-ee-ee-ee!" everyone joins in,
laughing.

"YO DO LAYEE-EE-EE-EE-EE!" spell the
fireflies.

And on this note the group turns and heads off again, away from the lake, around the shoulder of the long slope, and then up again, along a little rise. The fireflies flit ahead to the top and there, somewhat arrogantly, spell out, "SO GET A LOAD OF THAT," complete with italics and arrow.

Panting with effort, Rollo comes straining up ahead of Harv Tweetie. Beside the fireflies, he stops; he drops the equipment bag. He gawks.

"It's—it's—it's *Fairyland*!" he squawks.

The ground levels here, then slopes away again, way down to a sort of moat, with a little stone footbridge and a bright red rowboat alongside. There beyond rise the dense, darkened woods of some kind of island. A big billboard by the moat, jauntily floodlit, declares:

WELCOME TO FAIRYLAND— MIND YOUR STEP!

Is it all a trap? Are wrinkly, sharp-eyed kidnappers watching right now, from among the booby chutes in those dark woods?

It awaits a hero's courage to solve these lurking mysteries, that's what!

There in his Jellyfish uniform shirt, samurai swordstick in hand, Rollo gazes down beaming at the country of his quest. "This'll show Noreen where to get off, *forever*!" he announces. And he gulps, nervous, which is only natural. But thrilled.

Let's give him a few moments of triumph, while they last.

Fifteen

Question: Sure, ChooeyGooeys are super, if you're gaga for sugar; and Cremo-Crud Bars are a treat, too. But what is it that makes NuttiNutz such a shockingly lip-smacking, throat-grabbing, always crowd-pleasing overload of indigestible delight?

Is it that classic mixed-up mix of honey-crusted pecans, peanuts, and almonds, all stuffed into hunks of luscious caramel gunk so sweet and sticky, your many fillings start to sizzle?

Or is it that fake milk-chocolate coating clogged with coconut shavings and crusty nutty tidbits that stick between your teeth, and make your multiple cavities squeal?

Why the question? Oh, you'll see.

Sixteen

"It's—*Fairyland*!" repeats Rollo, in triumphant delight still, there gazing from above.

"Yeah, *big* deal, *Fairyland*," singsong the false teeth, mocking. They mock from down below on the slope Rollo came up. Because Harv Tweetie has suddenly halted at the bottom. Because he doesn't look good, at all. He's gone very pale and sweat covers his entire face.

"Fairyland," he gulps hoarsely. His trembling bony fists are clenched. "Goblin treasure . . . the Curse of the Tweeties. . . ." He shoves a jumble of veggies into his mouth.

Rollo goes back a step and peers down

toward him. "Come *on*!" he cries impatiently,
waving him to hurry up.

Then his attention is taken by the fireflies.
They've stopped their gloating and now spell
out: "HEY, WE'RE NOT FREE, YOU
KNOW!"

"You mean, we have to pay?" says Rollo to
them.

"OK, FORGET IT, CHEAPO," they spell
back. "SO GOT ANYTHING EXTRA-
SWEET, MAYBE?"

"Uh, *maybe* . . ." says Rollo. Then he grins.
"Sure!" Because despite their imperfect manners,
he really does appreciate the fireflies' guiding
assistance in his quest. Also he's always happy to
have a chance to show off his prize candy bars—
even though the situation now is annoyingly
complicated. But he recalls how Su-chi Samurai
Swordboy brought prize bugs and insects for the
Astral Turtles, the ones who helped him across
the bottomless river, so he could hack the evil
Iron Warriors' watchdog to pieces in its sleep.

For these various reasons Rollo darts a glance
over his shoulder and hurriedly pulls off his

backpack and reaches into its sticky sweet interior. "How about some *NuttiNutz*?" he announces, in a whisper flush with pride.

With these fateful words, there on the verge of Fairyland, he furtively holds out two whole candy bars, to be generous. "But you gotta taste them quick, 'cause—"

"Heedless criminal nitwit!" thunders Harv Tweetie's voice. *"What are you doing?"*

Rollo spins around, to see the adventurer emerging onto the top of the slope. And staring at Rollo, aghast. "Why, I'm just—" Rollo gulps, trying to pretend it's no big deal.

"Hoo boy," cry the false teeth. "Somebody say 'NuttiNutz'? *Gimme!*"

"Mo, no!" squawks Harv Tweetie, as the teeth spring off their shoulder perch, and hurtle through the air, and pounce on Rollo's candy gift. And his thumb too.

"Ow!—" yelps Rollo.

"Grr," growl the NuttiNutz-nutty joke dentures, gnashing away at both thumb flesh and sweet treats.

"*WAHT HTE*—" misspell the fireflies.

"Desist!" shouts Harv Tweetie, spraying veggie bits as Rollo hops about trying to pry the fake false teeth off without getting his other hand bitten.

"Leggo, leggo!" squawks Rollo.

"Evil sicko, cease your assault!" shouts Harv Tweetie—as Rollo now tries just to fling the dentures off, like you would a baseball mitt with a tarantula in it. With a *clonk!* the teeth fly loose and bounce onto the ground. They lie there gorging away at both candy bars at once, non-stop, right through the wrapping.

"Don't— *Mo!*" cries Harv Tweetie, hands twisting up in horror at the sight.

"My *thumb*," yelps Rollo. *"Ow!"*

At which point unfortunately, the fireflies get into the act. They swarm over the gnoshing teeth. They cover it like a coating of electrified nut tidbits. The teeth rock and wobble and hop about, sizzling and flashing, trying to keep on gnoshing but also ward off the furious candy-crazy minihorde.

It's a strangely pretty sight, actually, but at the same time shocking, like an illuminated jack-o'-lantern going berserk.

Rollo gapes, mouth open. Harv Tweetie hops and flaps about uselessly, crying, "Desist! Desist!"

And then it's over. The fake false teeth lie there twitching, oozing scorched, partly chewed caramelly gunk, all clogged with dead fireflies—a few of which wink on even in death. What a mess!

"Mo . . . Oh, Mo!" bleats Harv Tweetie, distraught, down on his knees over the ravaged joke dentures. He keeps twisting his helmeted head away and fluttering his hands, against the lure of the sweet glop.

"Nngh, nngh," gurgle the false teeth faintly. "Don't feel . . . so good. . . . Ate . . . too much. . . ." And they drool pathetically.

"Yuck—*disgusting*," grimaces Rollo. And then he snorts. And then he laughs, aggressively, feeling the throb of his thumb. "He's gonna die—from *overeating*! Ha ha!" he laughs. "It's *disgusting*, ha ha ha!"

This outburst makes Harv Tweetie's head snap up. "Are you *insane?*"

"You know, just like Marv," gulps Rollo, taken aback, the way you are when you see the joke, but no one else does. He laughs again, lamely.

"Monstrous little loony bird," snarls Harv Tweetie. "You're *responsible* for this! Mo! Mo!"

"*I'm* responsible?" sputters Rollo. "*He* bit *me*!" He exhibits his thumb. "And he's the one who tried to eat everything! He's always picking on me!" Rollo adds, just to point out the general unfairness of things.

"Think . . . I'm a goner . . ." burble the false teeth. And they twitch, and hiccup weakly, oozing.

"No, Mo, no!" squawks the frantic adventurer. He writhes. He stares up at Rollo with his one eye. "You have to give him mouth-to-mouth!"

"*Me?*" cries Rollo, shrinking back in horror. "No way, *yuck*!"

"But I can't, I can't! Not with such delicious chocolatey goop everywhere!" cries Harv Tweetie, twisting this way and that in the agony of resisting his curse. "Then get something to wipe him with!" he gasps. "So's we can carry him back to the ambulance and speed him to urgent medical care. Mo, Mo, you're gonna be fine!"

Rollo looks shocked. Because he is. "But— wait. What about Fairyland? And my quest?" He looks toward the big billboard rising right there down below, just on the other side of the moat.

"Curses on Fairyland! And your silly quest! Now get me something—look in the equipment bags!"

Rollo regards him, stunned. "No!"

"Sick, evil!" hisses Harv Tweetie. His one eye glares in a truly menacing way. *Want his death on your hands? Look in the bags, I tell you!*

"I don't care about his death on my hands," grumbles scowling Rollo. But he tries the bags as ordered, his shocked brain trying to comprehend the turn of events. "Well, I can't open the bags!" he announces. "All these straps are all asinine." Which is true. "Why don't you use your scarf?"

"More insanity!" retorts the adventurer. "This scarf's special prison property. Run back to the ambulance, there's some towels I snitched. Go on, hurry!"

"No!" protests Rollo. And he even stamps his foot.

"And mind your step on the way," the adventurer adds, not paying attention. "Oh, Mo!" he cries, in fresh woe, his fists clenched by his mouth.

And this is how Rollo finds himself hurrying in the starlight back down the slope he came up—*away* from Fairyland, *away* from his noble rescue quest, his steps carrying him back among the dangers of booby chutes, thank you. All because of the joke dentures' gluttonous greediness! "It's not *fair*," he complains aloud, as the light of the big moon gleams on his Jellyfish uniform shirt. And gleams across Pleasant Lake, spread out again below. His older sister's disrespecting sneers fill his ears. Just when he's so close! And then he stops. Because he realizes Harv Tweetie typically forgot to give him the car keys to unlock the ambulance!

With a curse, Rollo heaves around and clambers back muttering up the slope. He reaches the top, and then he jerks to a stop again—from horror.

Harv Tweetie has Rollo's open backpack beside him.

And he's wiping.

Seventeen

"*That's my* Su-ichi Samurai Swordboy *comic!*" squeals Rollo, in disbelief. Not to mention fury and outrage and hurt.

He rushes forward.

"Eh? You're back, where's the towels?" says Harv Tweetie, looking up while tearing out a fresh page of *manga* comic, as Rollo comes charging toward him. "Better than nothing, this, but I really requi—"

"*Gimme that!*" roars Rollo, and he snatches at the remains of the comic book in Harv Tweetie's grasp.

The nursing adventurer squawks in protest.

And hangs on! There's an actual tug-of-war—which Rollo wins, ripping free what's left of his beloved, treasured action *manga*.

"What are you doing!" he wails, gaping around at the crumpled pages scattered about on the ground, laden with NuttiNutz gunk and firefly carcasses and disgusting spit.

"Trying to save a life!" shouts Harv Tweetie. "Gimme the silly comic, *get back to the ambulance*!" He lunges flapping at Rollo's hands, but Rollo jerks the comic remains out of range.

"Don't feel . . . so good . . ." gurgle the joke dentures.

"It's just not fair!" wails Rollo, yet again, at the top of his lungs. This fairness line is turning into a real theme. Suddenly he rushes over to his hockey stick lying on the ground. He rushes back.

"I'm going!" he snarls, menacing Harv Tweetie while also clutching the precious comic book remnants under his arm, for safety. *"Gimme the map!—to Fairyland, I mean!"*

Harv Tweetie snorts, contemptuously. "The

map?" he laughs. "You're *mad*. You'll never be able to decipher— *No-o-o!*" he screeches.

As Rollo's whack, not quite accurate because of his emotional state, sends the pigged-out false teeth skittering away.

"Gimme the map!" roars Rollo, in the most ferocious of voices.

"*Sick*est—*evil*est—!" Harv Tweetie leaps to his feet. He scuttles a step toward the joke dentures. *"Mo! Mo!"* he blurts. He whirls around, scarf flapping. "I should *never* have listened to a depraved fiend like you! Oh, what a fool I was! I shoulda tormented you like I planned, oh, I shoulda!"

And he rushes over to his long goblin net on the ground as Rollo chases after him. He snatches the net up and whirls around again, brandishing the net pole upside down, handle end up. The handle is wrapped in hardened leather.

"You'll not touch the map—you'll go not one step farther! *'Cause I'm gonna hurt ya!*" he snarls. And he begins circling Rollo, leather-handled net pole raised to strike.

There overlooking Fairyland, in the starlight,

guide and young noble quester facing off, mortal enemies now!

Rollo gulps. A realization thrills him. This is exactly like the showdown between Su-ichi Samurai Swordboy and the treacherous Ghoul Wizard who impersonated the trusty old blind Dragon Scout! Rollo laughs, frightened but brave with fury. Hurriedly he stuffs away what's left of his beloved comic book under his Jellyfish shirt. This is as good as any dream, for an action-comics lover—an outraged action-comics lover! Why, it's a *manga* scene come to life. . . .

NOT EXACTLY SAMURAI-STYLE HEROICS, IS IT?

129

131

"Where'd he go?" sputter the double Tweeties.

They whirl around.

"He's escaping—to Fairyland!" roars Harv.

"Come back, you sneak!" squawks Marv's ghost. And it wails, *"AY-Y-Y!!"*

Ghost and adventurer give chase down the long slope after the scampering figure in a Jellyfish uniform shirt.

Rollo glances back as he desperately hurries along, with his backpack and hockey stick and the surviving pages of his gunked-up comic book. "I don't need a map," he grunts to himself, defiantly. "'Cause nothing's gonna stop me from my quest!"

Even if it means running off from a samurai-style showdown!

"Flog off his ears, flog off his nose!" yells Harv Tweetie's voice from behind.

Another ghostly wail goes up.

Rollo strains along faster. Ahead towers the Fairyland sign, right across the moat.

The cute stone bridge goes right across, with the rowboat beside it. Just as he's about to reach the bridge, Rollo spots the cozy sign, "**Right Across Here!**"—and he veers away, toward the rowboat. Because he's no *crafty* guide, but he knows a thing or two now, thank you! Of course he can't row, but he can use the rowboat as a kind of bridge, since the moat is so narrow. He looks back a last time at the chasing furious Tweeties. He laughs. Then he turns and leaps into the rowboat.

Which isn't a rowboat.

"No—" squawks Rollo, lurching to the sounds of splintering. *"No!"* he repeats—and then he disappears, flailing, down a booby chute.

Eyte
ihen

Meanwhile . . .

"I hope Piggy Sugarface isn't around," sniffs Renee Duffman, referring unkindly to a certain person as she troops in through Noreen's front door. They've had an evening's entertainment roaming the movieplex.

"No, thank *God*, he's off, I dunno, *somewhere*," drawls Noreen. And she yawns, in the most phony blasé way. "Face probably stuck in that stupid *Suzie Something* comic of his."

"Oh, God, *please*," snorts Renee, in disdain.

"Hey . . ." says Noreen. "Did I just get the

greatest idea? . . ." She grins, a wicked, mysterious grin.

"Like what?"

"Like, he'll find out . . ." gloats wicked Noreen. And she sniggers. "Wherever he's lurking. . . ."

Nineteen

Down, down the booby chute rockets screaming Rollo, at a steep angle, in darkness, minutes on end. His hockey-stick blade jams into his cheek, his backpack crams into his neck. Then his whole body seems to squash into his stomach, like at the bottom of a ride at Roaring Rainbows theme park. And then he's shooting back upward, through darkness. *"Whoa whoa whoa!"* gasps Rollo—and he slams into splintering wood and through it, and shoots out into fresh air. And bangs right into something.

And then plunges back down—a moment, before jerking to a violent stop.

"*Ungh*," groans Rollo, swaying, blinking at little spinning stars.

And is this how he finds himself sprawled in the branch of a tree?

Tweetny

Yup. Close enough.

Technically, and luckily, dangling by his backpack, which got caught on a stump of branch jutting from a low bough of a big tree—right under the bough into which he banged when he shot up out of the booby chute.

Whose dark, splintered mouth gapes, hungry for his return, four feet below.

"Help—" blurts Rollo at the sight; and thrashing away from it, he hears the branch stump crack, and he goes floundering, yelling, down toward the ground. He thuds down on top of his hockey stick—one leg in the dreaded booby chute.

"Help!" he squawks. Frantically he scrambles out. And he huddles over against the base of the tree, gasping, feeling at his scraped nose, ears and elbows, and yanked-about neck and shoulders.

"Wh-where am I?"

Apparently across the moat, in Fairyland, somewhere.

Fairyland—*at last*! *"Co-o-o-ol-esstt!"* is what questing Rollo would have expected to burst out with now, in self-congrats. And then something very pointed and personal about his sneering older sister. But the expected words just fade from his lips. He gulps.

Because all around him, from what he can see from under his tree, lies dark forest . . . the dark forest he gazed at earlier from a distance. Not entirely dark though, because of moonlight and starlight . . . and because of the little mischievous signs aglow here and there among the bushes and tree trunks, advertising "**New to Fairyland? Lean Here!**" or "**Enjoy Fairyland!** *Sit There!*" or "**Attaboy, Nice and Soft for Lying on, Fairyland-style!**"

"Jeepers," mumbles Rollo.

He grips his trembling hockey stick, and gets up, and inches forward a couple of brave steps, and peers out. He now sees paths, zigzagging away into the vast leafy dimness in a jumble of directions. "**Here Ya Go, Fairyland-goer!**" and "**Shortcut—Fairyland Approved!**" entice the signs. The whole place is like a crazy minimall and a mad traffic circle, all plunked into dark woods.

Amid eerie silence. There are no noises, Rollo realizes; no more shouts of the Tweetie twins.

He's all alone.

All alone and lost, at night, in a dark booby-chuted forest, without a map or any idea where he is, or what dangers exactly lie all around him: not only goblins, wild animals . . . *monsters* . . .

"M-m-mom!" squawks Rollo—to be honest, as much a plea as anything.

Silence.

"M-m-mom!"

And then he jumps, because somewhere a bird cackles. And then he jumps again, because of rustling in the bushes, near a big red toad-stool (*a big red toadstool*!). Rollo stares, frozen. More rustling. *"H-hey,"* he gulps, hockey stick a-tremble. He backs up a step. Then he yelps and scurries back behind the tree, and peers out from there. A little face peeps out at him from under the toadstool: a squirrel's face. It blinks.

"St-stupid squirrel!" curses Rollo.

The squirrel blinks again, then disappears, noisily. Something hoots high up in the tree branches.

Rollo huddles, cowering in his Jellyfish shirt and his backpack. Not so heroic, to be blunt about it. Some kids are great fans of the dark, but he's not one of them. He once survived four minutes alone in his empty house with the lights off, on a bet. Which he lost, because the bet was fifteen minutes. His heart pounds now, and he moans, softly, so as not to attract attention. Softly, softly he opens the wrapping of a NuttiNutz Bar and nibbles, just to try to feel better. How creepy, the demented way some people have behaved on account of his beloved treat.

Then he tries to squint at his surviving pages of *Su-ichi Samurai Swordboy*, for spiritual buck-up and guidance, as always. But the pages are dishearteningly sticky from you-know-what. *"I'm glad if I killed the sickening false teeth,"* Rollo mumbles, bitterly. "Oh, but what am I going to do, oh, I'm so scared," he whimpers (no other word for it). Harv Tweetie was right, he'll never find his way to where the goblins hang out! Hideous Noreen was right, everything's a colossal mess! He's all alone, lost in the dark, dark forest!

Plainly, Rollo's losing it. All heroes have their difficult moments; this sure is his.

"Oh, I wish I weren't all alone," Rollo moans away, rocking back and forth now. "Oh, I wish I had someone here with me—someone like Su-ichi Samurai Swordboy! Oh, I wish *he* was here! Oh, I *wish*, I *wish*!" You get the idea. And back and forth he rocks, clutching the disrespected comic pages to his chest, squeezing his eyes shut, *wishing, wishing* for heroic *manga*-inspired help in the dark lonely forest of Fairyland.

Something rustles next to him. His eyes snap open—he jolts back, with a squawk, dropping the comic book remains—

146

"But what's wrong with me?" says Soupy
Songboy, looking hurt. "I'm lots of fun; I can
sing! Listen, it'll cheer you up. *Tra-la-la, Tra-la-
la!*" he croons, strumming the ukulele in his
Hawaiian shirt. He's awful.

"You're *awful*," Rollo snarls.

"What a mean thing to say!" blurts the songboy, and his chubby face crumples as if he was
going to cry. Then he cringes as something hoots
loudly overhead. "What was that?" he gulps. He
peers up and around, in distress. "Gee, it's awful

spooky here, I can see why you were scared!"

"I wasn't *scared*!" Rollo informs him savagely. "And my name is *Rollo*! And don't you know *anything* about being a samurai?"

"'Course not, I'm an entertainer!" whines Soupy Songboy in his little straw hat. "Don't blame me, I'm just the creation of your imagination—blame yourself!"

"But how're you going to help me in my noble quest? And rescue my mom from the goblins?"

"What're *goblins*?" says the flabby one. Before Rollo can scream, he adds, "How about a map? Maybe that's one, will that help?"

And he pushes Rollo enough to waggle loose a piece of paper Rollo seems to have been sitting on.

It's a map.

Twenty-One

"Where'd *that* come from?" squawks Rollo.

"I dunno, you were sitting on it," says Soupy Songboy. "Hey—" he yelps as Rollo tries to snatch the map from him. The map tears in half. "You're so rude!" he cries, as Rollo now grabs both pieces.

Rollo stares at what he has in his hands. Where *did* it come from? It looks just like his glimpse of Harv Tweetie's (and Officer Ronizoni's) map of Fairyland, except this copy displays the NuttiNutz logo, which he hadn't noticed before. And besides being torn, the paper is mushed, from his sitting on it. But there's the same tortured tangle of dotted paths shown winding about . . . and among them, one path is specially marked in some kind of code, leading to "Goblins' Hangout!"

"That's *complicated* code," grumbles the Imaginary Friend, peering. "What's 'ereH gnolapoH' mean? Hey, where're you going?"

Rollo crawls away to the edge of the tree branches. He stares out, map parts in hand. He jumps to his feet.

"That's the one, that's it!" he yells wildly, pointing off at a path whose very little sign reads very simply, as if trying to stay unnoticed, "Hopalong Here." *"Hopalong Here!"* laughs Rollo. The map just had it spelled backward. Now really, how hard was that to decipher? What a ridiculous phony, Harv Tweetie, and his specialized map-reading wisdom!

Except, Rollo now realizes, there's another "Hopalong Here" sign on another path. And on another. "Three of them?" mumbles Rollo, confused.

"That's *confusing*," protests the flabby songboy. "We better just stay here, it's much safe— *What was that!*" he squawks, jerking around as something hoots from nearby.

"Quit doing that!" Rollo hisses, spooked by his companion's jumpiness.

"Well, it's *scary*!"

"Quit *saying* that!" It's maddening when you're struggling to control your emotions, and someone just splashes theirs around all over the place.

"Well, if you won't let me sing to comfort myself, how about something to eat?"

"But you're imaginary!" retorts Rollo. "You don't eat!"

"'Course I eat, everybody *eats*!" whines Soupy Songboy. Really, does he love to play the victim! Just the sort of company you need, lost at night in a dark wilderness—*hardly. "I'm starving!"*

"Well, I guess you can maybe have a NuttiNutz Bar," scowls Rollo, grudgingly. Not wanting to share in the least, and also uneasy, after the disaster earlier. "But only one, 'cause—"

"Only *one*? But I love NuttiNutz. Gimme me four!"

"No!"

"Ye-e-es!"

"Know what?" Rollo announces. "I think your being here is a big mistake—*I think you should go back to where you came from!"*

"You are so *rude*!" whimpers the imaginary songboy. "No!" he sniffs, defiantly. "I won't go!" And he crosses his arms in his Hawaiian shirt.

What a mess.

"What d'you *mean*?" sputters Rollo. "I *created* you! So I'm ending you!"

"So what, I refuse. And if you're not going to give me enough to eat to comfort myself, at least let me sing!" And he grabs up his ukulele and strums it.

"Stop that, stop it! *Go away!*" Rollo yells at him, coming toward him, clenching his fists.

"You're *so mean*! *Bwwa-wwa!*" blubbers Soupy Songboy, hugging his ukulele.

The whole thing's just unbearable!

"Okay!" shouts Rollo, wild eyed, at wit's end. *"So guess what—then I'll go!"* And he stamps over to get his backpack and hockey stick and partial comic book.

Except the blubberer flops at him and grabs him around the knees and hangs on like a kid who doesn't want to go to first day of school.

"You can't, it's *so scary* here, don't leave me!" he wails.

"Leggo, *leggo*!" cries Rollo, enraged at the monstrous nightmare his scheming older sister has created. He shoves and tugs at the clutching songboy, who feels weirdly squishy and foggy. *"Ow ow!"* cries the squishy clutcher. With an immense heave, Rollo sends him back *sproing!* onto his ukulele—and partway down into the mouth of the booby chute. *"H-help—"* Soupy squawks, floundering. He flounders even more as our noble-hearted Rollo now actually tries to force his unwanted Imaginary Friend down the splintery hole! But the oversize songboy won't go in, he clings and clasps.

"Just—*go! Let go!*" splutters Rollo. Finally he just wrenches away in frustration and stalks over to grab his things, and stamps off—but not before having to dodge yet another of Soupy's flopping clutches!

"Don't leave me. I'm *so-o scared*!" bawls the fatso songboy, stretched out pathetically on the ground.

"Shut up shut up!"

And thanks to all this insanity Rollo turns, and goes stomping out recklessly through the leafy darkness, toward the mischievously glowing signs.

Twenty-Two

Fast as he dares, Rollo stalks along, his heart thumping, his eyes darting about for booby chutes. From the bottom of his soul he curses his older sister. He makes it to the first path marked "Hopalong Here." Where he stops. He gulps. He squints at the scraps of map; but really, it's all like a practical joke! The path winds away into Fairyland, between trees with huge flat leaves like from a kids' picture book he once had . . . to where, though, and to what? *"Jeepers,"* complains Rollo. He curses again. He sniffs at the air for goblin smell. He takes a timid first brave step. He hears his obnoxious Imaginary

Friend carrying on behind in the distance.

Or not the distance?

He spins around—and to his horror, sees Soupy Songboy coming tottering after him, both arms outstretched in front, like a massive toddler rushing after its mom.

"No!" cries Rollo. "Go away—*you're gonna screw up my quest!*"

"Wait! I'm coming with you! *Bwwa-wwa!*"

"*No!*" screeches Rollo. "Stop—" Furiously he waves his hockey stick. He looks desperately this way and that. Then he just bolts off down the path—just to get away from this clutching Frankenstein monster! He scrambles along, frantically trying to watch out for little tricky signs and glossy surprise patches. What a fiasco his arrival in Fairyland has turned into! "I *hate* Noreen, I *hate* her," sputters Rollo. (Like we didn't know.)

"*Bwwa-wwa!*" bawls the Imaginary Friend, somewhere off behind.

The path curves—then suddenly forks in two. "*Jeepers—*" Rollo jams to a halt. He has no idea which way to go. Then he hears a most wonderful sound—the sound of shrieking.

"It's another hole—I'm *stuck*!" shrieks Soupy Songboy's voice. "He-e-elp, I'm *falling in*!"

Rollo comes a step back up the path, beaming. "A booby chute! *Ha ha*, have a nice ride!"

"Oh, please help me! *Bwwa-wwa!*"

"Ask Noreen to help! *Ha ha!*"

He turns away gleefully, his ears full of pitiful wailing—and then he gulps. At a sudden smell. And he jolts back, gawking at a bush near the path.

A wrinkly, sharp-eyed little face gawks back at him.

"Goblin!—" Rollo sputters. (At last!) Fumbling he jerks up his hockey stick.

The goblin in his bushy flowery jacket looks wildly from side to side, hesitating. Because, it's now clear, he's in the midst of peeing. With a yelp he suddenly tries to scramble away into the bushes, but hopping and hobbling awkwardly, trying to straighten his leaf-thatched pants but still not finished with his business.

"Stop!" roars Rollo. "Or I'll slap-shot your block off!"

The goblin halts, cowering and fumbling with himself.

"Gross—" blurts Rollo. About the mess and the smell.

"That's not n-nice!" squeaks the little goblin, trembling, his ugly face curdling like he's going to start whining. "You b-big b-bully."

"I'm not a bully!" snorts Rollo. "So where's my mom?" His heart pounds with excitement. "I'm Rollo Samurai Stickboy and I'm here to rescue her and you're my hostage! I order you to take me to her!" And then he turns his head to shout at Soupy Songboy, who's been keeping up his obnoxious wailing the whole time, like a car alarm.

"See? A b-big bully," whimpers the little goblin. "A big one."

"I'm not a bully!" exclaims Rollo. Really, this is like a ludicrous bad dream. "I'm actually courageous and brave and noblehearted, okay? You're the ones who kidnapped my mom! Wait a minute—" he gulps suddenly, with a rush of concern, "are the rest of the goblins around here?" He twists about, hockey stick at the ready.

"No, they're all back at the Goblins' Hang-out."

"Is that where you've got her? She better be unharmed—you better not have tortured her! "

"She's *fine*," protests the goblin. "But she's so *bossy*, she keeps making that lumpy awful banana crème pie, I'm gonna throw up."

"My mom's not bossy!" retorts Rollo, defending his family honor against outsiders (even if their criticism is true). "And that pie is *delicious*! So you—you take me to her, and no tricks! *Shut up!*" he screams back down the path at the blubbering and wailing.

"No, I won't, I won't—I'm never going back!" squeals the goblin—and he scurries off again in little prancing steps. Rollo yells and chases after him. Round and round another bush they go, the goblin cringing and clattering like a runaway kindergartner, his long wrinkly ears and little wrinkly hands flapping in the air. Finally he cowers to a quaking, trembly stop. On a scale of ferocity, he ranks so far below the goblin horde at Pleasant Lake, it's a joke. As a questing hero's worthy adversary, such as a Ghost

Demon Assassin, he's an out-and-out disaster.

"Oh, please, I'm just trying to get out of Fairyland, I can't take her anymore, I tell you, she's so bos"—("She's *not* bossy!")—"and all that sugar and starch and the booby chutes and signs and paths, I'm too sensitive, I'm going mad, it's *so stressful!*" the goblin bleats. And it's true, dark shadows ring his eyes, a sure sign of terrible stress. "I don't know how to get to the Goblins' Hangout, I'm lost, the map is so *confusing.*" He fumbles out a map from his jacket and holds it up in both hands, pathetically.

Rollo blinks at it. It's just like the map he has. "Where did you get that?" he squawks.

"They gave them away with jumbo giant packs of those—those *evil* NuttiNutz Bars. They're all over the place."

To his amazement, Rollo now sees copies of the Fairyland map scattered about in the undergrowth. "Huh? But what d'you, what d'you mean *evil* NuttiNutz? Nuttinutz are the greatest! And I don't believe you don't know where your own Goblins' Hangout is—I command you to take me there, as my hostage! And, uh, *honestly,*"

159

he says, dropping his voice, "what *is* the goblin treasure, anyway?"

"No—never!" cries the little goblin, in torment. "I'll never break my oath and tell, I've said enough, they'll boil me with rotten acorns! And I can't take you to the Goblins' Hangout even if I wanted, 'cause I'm lost!"

"Well, at least you must know if *this* 'Hopalong Here' path goes there!"

"Maybe it does, maybe. . . ."

"Aw, *come on*—is it at least *near* here?"

"Maybe—I dunno. I'm *lost*, you bully!" squeals the cowering hostage.

"I'm not a bully," hisses Rollo, threatening with his hockey stick, at wit's end again. "I *order you* to take me to— *SHUT UP!!*" he roars over his shoulder.

"I'm never going back, I'll die first!" wails the goblin, rushing off. And before Rollo can stop him, he launches himself in a suicidal belly flop right onto a bunch of crudely shiny buttercups. With a last squeak and a splintery cracking, he disappears into the ragged hole in the ground.

And then except for a bushy jacket sleeve

that got caught in the splinters, Rollo is all alone again.

Not quite.

"I got out, it was so *scary*, where are you? Don't leave me!" bawls a distant voice.

"No! *No*—" sputters Rollo. He comes scrambling back out onto the path. He hesitates. What to do, what to do? He twists left, right. Cursing, he heads on toward where the path forks. Which fork to take? He tries frantically to make sense of the map scraps. But what's the use? "Mom!" he shouts, and rushes down the left fork, just to go somewhere.

Whereupon a honeysuckle-covered log by the path ahead jiggles, and explodes.

Twenty-Three

And into the Fairyland moonlight erupt two bony, writhing figures, one dim and ghostly, one in an explorer's helmet, with a long net between them.

"The Tweeties!" gasps Rollo. He lurches to a stop.

The twins plunge back toward their booby chute—and then, using the net pole to jam their reentry, they tumble down beside it.

With a curse, Rollo spins around, and goes rushing back up where he came. He reaches where the path forked; he takes the other choice. This path curves too, little leering signs aglow beside it. Rollo charges on and on around—then screeches to a halt. *"No—"* Because the path has wound around right back to the booby chute hole and the Tweeties! Who are up and peering around, one eyed.

"There he is!" cries Harv Tweetie. "The fiendish sicko!"

"Flog off his ears, flog off his nose!" wails Marv Tweetie's ghost.

"Get *Jellybeanieweaniemeanie*!" sneers the dim, ghostly blob on Harv Tweetie's shoulder.

And they charge after Rollo, who's spun around and gone dashing off back along where he came. *This is all screwed up—*" he pants. Which is a fact and then some. He races along, absolutely reckless now, making desperately for the fork in the path— and skids to a halt.

Because down the curving path comes tottering at long last a certain Hawaiian shirt.

"Bwwa-wwa!" bawls its owner, monstrous arms outstretched. *"Bwwa-wwa!"*

"No, wait—wait, my *quest*—" sputters Rollo, twisting this way and that as his multiple antagonists close in. Cornered! Desperately he turns round and round. *"Mom!"* he squawks. *"Mom!"*

There's a rough stone wall in the dark undergrowth across the path. With a gap in it.

And at least no glowing signs. Who knows what lies beyond? With a frantic cry, Rollo plunges through the gap to get away.

Except it's not a gap. He slams into trick-painted stone wall—*ow!*—and bounces off, and careens sprawling down onto the path, hockey stick flying.

"**Whoops**," a little sign lights up.

"*Layee-ee-ee, Yo do lo!*" a muffled voice yodels, somewhere nearby . . . below?

"No—" With a gasp Rollo manages to roll away, just as a tuft of grass bursts open, and Officer you-know-who blasts up into the Fairyland moonlight. Followed by the suicidal goblin, minus a jacket sleeve! Followed by the furious magic-store owner!!

The noise of bad yodeling and *"It's all so stressful,"* and "Stop! Thief!" mixes with the chaos of bawls and yells clamoring in from both sides.

"Wait—*my quest*—" sputters Rollo, thrashing and struggling, about to be overwhelmed or go mad. Or both.

At which point a figure steps out of the trees, and peers down at him.

Twenty-four

"Mom—" blurts Rollo—as his eyes blink open.

"Rollo!" exclaims his mother.

She's not in the forest. She's in the door of his bedroom. In daylight.

"Rollo, what are you doing on the *floor?*" she demands. "What's going on? Noreen said she heard so much yelling and shouting from in here, she was actually *alarmed*!"

"Probably brain poisoning from all those candy bars he sucks down," sneers Noreen, beside her.

Rollo gawks at them from the carpet where he's lying. In his pajamas. "Ungh?" he says.

"Kindly *hurry up*, Rollo!" orders his mother. "It's a long drive up to Pleasant Lake, we're already late because of you. We want to be able to enjoy the fireflies at supper."

Rollo blinks at her.

"We didn't already go to Pleasant Lake?" he says. In the oddest little voice.

"What's the matter with his voice?" sneers Noreen.

"What are you *talking* about, Rollo, we're going up today!" snaps his mother. "Are you still dreaming or something? *What are you doing, pinching yourself like that!"*

"Told you he was insane," announces Noreen.

"He must be *insane!*" his dad agrees, a few minutes later, downstairs in the kitchen. Because Rollo's there speaking again in the same odd voice, this time to refuse going up to Pleasant Lake. "It's our family outing!" his dad informs him. "Your mom's made her 'family favorite' banana crème pie!"

"Not going," repeats Rollo, simply.

"What *manners*," harrumphs his mom. "Fine. Suit yourself. Just consider yourself grounded."

"Yeah, for the whole month," says his father.

"Okay."

"And no more candy bars," adds his mother.

Rollo gulps. "Okay."

"And take away his stupid *Suzie Something* comic book!" adds Noreen.

"You just shut up!" screeches Rollo, glaring at her. Then he just shrugs. "Okay."

"Rollo, what has gotten into you!" says his mom. She shakes her head.

The rest of the family loads up the van and drive off an hour later, to Pleasant Lake.

"And why is he *smiling* like that?" are Noreen's last sneering words, which Rollo hears as he watches from the back steps. He's been restricted to the house.

Yes, Rollo smiles. But very carefully. For the next hour, he tiptoes through the house, testing the carpets and stairs for surprises. To his relief, there are none. Then he cleans up his room, at least much of it, as ordered. His cleaning sets a new standard for him. He stuffs his Jellyfish uniform shirt and his hockey stick deep, deep into the back of his closet.

Then down in the living room, he just sits, having been forbidden TV or music.

His candy bars have been confiscated. So has his *Su-ichi Samurai Swordboy* comic book. You know what?

He doesn't miss it.

Because he has had it with quests.

Every once in a while, he pinches himself. And when nothing happens, he gives a little laugh . . . carefully.

By late afternoon, he summons the courage to go out onto the front porch . . . cautiously.

Whereupon he gulps.

Who should come walking by the mailbox but Mrs. Schnockler and her doggie, Snowflake.

She stops. "Hello, Raleigh," she announces. "Saw your folks and your sister earlier today, off to Pleasant Lake. What's the matter, not feeling well?"

"I'm okay," answers Rollo, after a pause.

"My, you sound odd," says Mrs. Schnockler. "And why—why are you staring at Snowflake like that? Stop it, you'll spook him!"

On cue Snowflake in his red bow starts yapping away frantically at Rollo.

"See!" says Mrs. Schnockler, annoyed. "And why're you *grinning* like that now? Honestly, you're a *strange* boy, Raleigh!" And with that she lurches away at the end of the leash.

"It's Rollo," murmurs Rollo, watching them go.

But yes, he's grinning. And then beaming, in fact—no longer carefully. Because, sure, doggie Snowflake is obnoxious.

But he's just a doggie!

In a wave of relief, Rollo slips a hand into his pocket and wiggles out the special NuttiNutz Bar he always keeps hidden for emergencies. And he rewards himself with a slow, delicious, tooth-buzzing mouthful. Really now, could such a sweet treat be the cause of *anything* but joy and happiness? And then he hears high-pitched barking, and Snowflake comes bounding back around the street corner, trailing his leash. He comes bounding up to Rollo's mailbox, and then down the path, right up to the porch steps. He barks up at Rollo, wiggling his little pom-pom tail.

Mouth open, frozen midchew, Rollo stares down. A terrible sinking feeling slowly engulfs him. It speeds up as Snowflake grins and says: "Hey, wanna know what the goblin treasure is?

Just the world's most jumbo giant secret stash of amazing NuttiNutz Bars—like from your wildest dreams! *Cool, huh?*" says the doggie with his red bow.

"*Jeepers . . .*" declares Rollo. In a very faint, very odd voice; not just because his mouth is full. Not a happy voice, really, at all.

"Of course you know what they say about candy," continues Snowflake.

It's from this moment on that Rollo decides never to eat another candy bar in his life, and to learn to love broccoli, and zucchini, and every other healthy vegetable.

But, unfortunately, as you've probably guessed, it's much too late for that.

"Yo do layee-ee-ee-ee-ee, Yo do lo!"

Anya von Bremzen

NASTY but true! Writer-performer Barry Yourgrau wrote *NASTYbook*, the first in the *NASTYbooks* series. "Very funny . . . and magnificently nasty," harrumphed author Neil Gaiman. Kids all over have screamed (outrage) and laughed and gulped (horror) when Barry's read aloud at their schools. Barry has a history of startling performances, on MTV and NPR—even in a rock-music video he starred in. He won a Drama-Logue award for performing his book *Wearing Dad's Head*. He's also acted in Hollywood films—as a bee-stung high school principal and a scary-scary scientist.

"With *Another NASTYbook*," whispers Barry, "here's a whole novel that's nastily demented—maybe too demented for you??" We won't be tricked into answering! But wait: can there be more NASTYness lurking ahead—a third *NASTYbook*? You'll have to see, won't you. . . .

Born in South Africa, Barry came to the U.S. as a kid . . . a very strange kid. Keep up to date on all his NASTY mischief—check out www.nastybook.com and Barry's own website, www.yourgrau.com. And listen to his *NASTYbook* audiobook.